GRAB BAG
Two Books

BY DEREK McCORMACK

BROOKLYN, NEW YORK

**Also from Dennis Cooper's
LITTLE HOUSE ON THE BOWERY series**

Victims
a novel by Travis Jeppesen

Headless
stories by Benjamin Weissman

The Fall of Heartless Horse
by Martha Kinney
(forthcoming)

This is a work of fiction. All names, characters, places, and incidents are the product of the author's imagination. Any resemblance to real events or persons, living or dead, is entirely coincidental.

Published by Akashic Books
©2004 Derek McCormack

ISBN: 978-1-888451-59-7
Library of Congress Control Number: 2003116592

All rights reserved
Second Akashic Books printing

Little House on the Bowery
c/o Akashic Books
Instagram, X, Facebook: AkashicBooks
info@akashicbooks.com
www.akashicbooks.com

The author thanks Dennis Cooper, Sam Hiyate, Hilary McMahon, Ian Phillips, Johnny Temple, and Joel Westendorf.

Dark Rides *is dedicated to the McCormack family—*
Cynthia, Melissa, and Murray.
Wish Book *is dedicated to Jason McBride.*
Grab Bag *is dedicated to Ken Sparling.*

DARK RIDES
A Novel in Stories

BACKWARD

I hid in my room. Scrubbed sand on my pecker and belly and bum. I was trying to kill the germs but my hands kept shaking and then it hit me. The man's word. *Combust*.

* * *

The ground smoked. The police come by. Also a man in a black suit who talked to Dad and the firemen.

I said to him, "You find out who done it?"

He said nobody did it. He said germs lived in our hay and rotted it and the rotting made it hot. He said it was chemical. He called it something.

"What do you mean germs?" I said.

"They're invisible," he said. "You can't get rid of them."

Grab Bag

* * *

The roof crashed and sparks flew up. A firetruck roared in. Behind it come a truck loaded up with guys.

Dad shook me by the shoulders. He said, "What were you doing?" He said, "Were you fooling with caps?"

I started to cry. My snot all black from smoke.

* * *

Dad dove into the smoke. Then him and the horses come barrelling out. McNaughtons drove down from their farm and then the Pointers run down from theirs and they all got a water line going between the barn and the well. Me holding buckets while Ted Pointer pumped.

Ted shouted, "You didn't see anyone did you?"

I shook my head. The flames went high as pines.

* * *

The sun was burning something fierce. The grass

pricked my feet. I tiptoed to the stoop and plopped down on the porch glider, picked hayseed out of my hair and off my shoulders. Then I heard it. A whoosh. The barn blurred. Flames sawed the roof.

* * *

Ted Pointer was lying at the back of the hayloft. "How's my buddy?" he said.

The hay was cooking. I stepped out of my overalls and crouched. His pecker was jerking itself upright. Blue veins, green veins, veins the color of red cabbage. I put the end of it in my mouth. Horses snorting below. Then he lifted my head and rolled on top of me and started rubbing his body against mine. His forehead dripping into my eyes.

TREASURE TRAIL

I had to stand in a cornfield, arms spread scarecrow-style. Straw hat, cord suit. Wormy husks up my sleeves and down my neck.

Just past sundown a bunch of people rode by on a hay wagon.

A gal with a megaphone said, "Rumour has it Wendell hid out in these parts. He lived on berries and innocent children . . ."

I hollered and charged the wagon. Kids shrieked. Parents hugged them, pointed at me and laughed.

Every half hour another wagonload rumbled by. At 11 the driver drove down alone.

"I'm Pete," he said.

"Good for you," I said.

* * *

The megaphone gal gabbed about ghosts and ghouls as the first wagonload of the night rolled away.

I had a smoke. I jacked off. I wandered to the edge of the field and scaled the snake fence. Wading through tallgrass I tripped on a wheel. It was sticking straight up out of the ground. I found another one about five feet away. I began digging with my hands.

In the wagon Pete asked how I'd gotten dirty.

"You tell the boss and I'll kill you," I said.

He traced an X on his chest. "Cross my heart."

"There's a hay rake buried out there." I pointed.

"So?"

"So?" I said. "People'll pay lots for shit like that. It's an antique."

* * *

Next shift I took a shovel. I managed to unearth the rake's seat and prongs. But I had to keep running back to the cornfield to spook brats. One kid in snow pants started bawling. I rushed her. She grabbed my sleeve and chomped down on my fingers.

"Goddammit!" I yelled.

The boss was waiting by the barn after work. "Young man this is a family ride," he said. "Any more cussing and you're out of here! History! Understand?"

I hung my head. Out the corner of my eye I watched Pete park and lock the wagon.

* * *

"What a dope," Pete said next night. We passed a pasture planted with cardboard tombstones. "He didn't even ask what happened."

"Tell me something pal," I said. "The boss let you keep the keys to this thing?"

He shrugged. "Sure."

"Let's say you wanted to borrow it."

"No problem."

"Suppose you didn't ask."

The Haunted Barn, The Haunted Mini-Golf Course, The Haunted Snack Shack. Lights were out at the boss' house. A jack-o'-lantern asleep on the stoop.

* * *

Next shift I dug down to the rake's tongue. The soil beneath it was froze. I climbed onto the seat and jacked off.

The wagon rumbled closer.

I jammed my dick into my cords and ran. My right foot slid into a groundhog hole. I tumbled. The wagon's headlights grew bright.

"It seems the scarecrow's gone," said the megaphone gal. "Where could it be?"

"Here I am!" I yelled. I rose and staggered toward the wagon. "Here I am you fucking little bitch!"

Later on Pete idled the wagon beneath a rag-stuffed dummy dangling from an elm. He peeled off my boot and sock.

I faked a sob. "What am I gonna do?" I said. "I needed this job."

"This sucks," Pete said. "You hurt yourself making money for Mr. Moore. One little mistake and he's all over you." He slammed the gear stick into drive. "I'll help you get that rake," he said. "Just say when."

***

Halloween night I knocked out two sections of the snake fence. Near midnight Pete showed up in the wagon. We backed up to the rake, roped its rear beam to the wagon's hitch.

"I reckon it'll take one good tug," Pete said jumping into the cab.

The engine revved, the rope tensed, the rake groaned. *Crack!*—the beam snapped. Prongs and chunks of wood flew into weeds.

Pete leapt out. "Did we get it?" he said.

"Get it?" I screamed. "You fucking idiot you broke it!"

I slugged him in the kisser. He hit the dirt.

"C'mon candyass!" I screamed. "Get up and fight!"

Blood trickled from his nose.

"Pete?" I nudged him with my boot. Straddling his hips I pushed his sweater up to his armpits. I listened to his heartbeat. I licked his nipples. I unbuckled his belt.

WHEN IN ROME

> *Disguised in a wig Caligula roamed the streets of Rome, stabbing soldiers and dumping their bodies down sewers...*

In October my History teacher assigned presentations. My topic—the Emperor Caligula.

I asked the school librarian where I could find information. She brought me *The Twelve Caesars* by Suetonius. A clothbound edition made in Great Britain.

"This may not be removed from the library," she said, "but you're free to use it here."

I sat at a reading table and started making notes. Dates of Caligula's electoral reforms, military campaigns. How many consulships he took. Then I saw this:

> *Caligula was accused of homosexual relations, both active and passive, with Marcus Lepidus, and Mnester the comedian, and various foreign hostages...*

My cheeks flushed. I reread the sentence. I copied it out in capitals.

> *Caligula would force men to wear short tunics and run alongside his chariot...*

The next day I lunched in a carrel. I read how Caligula annexed parts of Rome for his palace. City blocks became hallways, tenements became suites. In one suite he opened a brothel. Men could go and sleep with the boys and married women who worked there.

Boys. My penis ballooned. Hands pocketed I rushed to the Tech hall washroom.

> *Caligula would invite men to supper, forgetting he'd murdered them already...*

When I got back to the library my books were gone. I ransacked my knapsack. I checked under my chair.

Someone snickered. A guy in the opposite carrel rose and waved Suetonius at me.

I walked around, heart trilling. The guy was sitting with another fellow who started reading my notes:

"Caligula was a queer accused of fucking every queer in Rome and als—"

I grabbed them. "Please give me the book," I said.

The first guy grinned and tossed it on the desk. Pressing its right side he yanked its left, splitting the spine.

Age eighteen Caligula loved watching tortures and executions . . .

I handed the book in to the librarian. The librarian dragged me to see the principal. I got detention for three weeks. After school I swept the gym. Student Council members were there, stringing orange and black streamers between the lights.

Caligula surveying a lineup of convicts: "Kill every man between the bald one and that short one!"

I bused to the Peterborough Public Library and

signed out another copy of *The Twelve Caesars*. All the way home I read. Every day Caligula ate doses of twenty-three poisons to build up his resistance. He wrote two books—one listed poisons and their effects, the other the names of people he'd poisoned. His own father died with foaming lips and dark blotches on his body.

Some convicts were stabbed forty or fifty times . . .

After supper Mom and Dad went to a movie. I nibbled a daffodil bulb, sucked petals from a potpourri. I fixed a rubbing alcohol and Coca-Cola cocktail. Caligula liked the taste of pearls dissolved in vinegar. I stirred an aspirin into my drink. It gave me pins and needles in my hands and feet. My eyes started focusing without me.

Some convicts were manacled and tossed into the Tiber . . .

Juiced up on poison I lit out for the school. Leaves cartwheeling down the sidewalk before me.

I slipped into the foyer, past kids bobbing for apples. In the gym a band was strumming a country song under the basketball hoop.

Others were dragged naked through the streets until stones sliced them and their bowels plopped out . . .

I hunted the fools who'd destroyed my library book. Through the cafeteria, the teacher's lunchroom, the parking lot. In the men's locker room I found three lugs straddling urinals.

"Check out the faggot," one lug said.

"You a fag?" said another.

"Hate me," I said, "so long as you fear me!"

They wrenched my arm and pulled my hair and dragged me on my knees into a stall. Piss frothing in the toilet.

"Thirsty fag?"

"I'm warning you," I said.

In I went. My forehead banged porcelain. I screamed as they pulled me out. I shut my mouth before they dunked me again.

THE CREPE-HANGER

I dumped the eye shadows on my bed—Midnight Mauve, Granite Gray, Satiny Silver.

"I'll look like a fairy!" Jack said. He huffed, lay down, unbuttoned his shirt. With my finger I smeared shadows on his neck, his chin. His lips.

My penis shot up. I crossed my legs.

Carved turnips grimacing from stoops. Maple trees red as clown wigs. I had on a lab coat and stethoscope. Jack in a Salvation Army suit, hair teased and greened with paint powder.

Jekyll and Hyde.

"Happy fucking Halloween," Jack mumbled.

A sheeted ghost hung from the Powells's porch light. Paula answered the door, a cat in cat-pattern slipover and silk whiskers.

"You must be Jack!" she said. "Happy Halloween!"

Black and orange serpentines crisscrossed the drawing room ceiling. Paula introduced us to her folks and some girls from out of town. The rest of the guests we knew. Gerry McBride was a jack-o'-lantern. Muslin stretched over a wire cage.

"Hey Jack," he said, "where's your costume?"

"Shut up pumpkin boy."

Mrs. Powell clapped. "How about a game?"

She split us into teams, placed us on opposite sides of a white sheet hanging in a doorway. All lights off. The other team flicked on a flashlight. A shadow loomed up on the sheet—broad shoulders, porcupine hair . . .

"Jack!" I yelled. I won a LifeSavers roll garnished with a crepe ruff bow tie.

They sent up Gerry the jack-o'-lantern next. The beam pierced the costume's muslin, silhouetted its frame. An X-ray of God knows what.

We went down to the cellar. On the ceiling skull-and-crossbones string-'em-outs, on the walls crepe moss. A banner over the buffet: *YE OLDE PIRATE'S CAVE.*

Paula pointed to the food. "We've got treasure chests—" She held up a platter of triple-decker brown bread sandwiches. "Pieces of eight—" Chocolate-chip cookies with gold frosting. "Ices, candies, cider . . ."

Jack held up a plate of chocolate croquettes. "What're these?" he said. "Pirate turds?"

Mr. Powell carried in a tin tub brimming with water and apples. Mrs. Powell in tow with towels. "Who wants to go first?" he said. "Derek? Dan? Gerry?"

"Oh for pete's sake," Jack said. He shucked his blazer, knelt at the tub. A deep breath and *splash!* He came up empty-mouthed. Next dip the powder in his hair became an emerald paint slick. He jerked up. "Get this crap out of my eyes!" he yelled.

Paula rushed him upstairs. Ten minutes later she led him down. His makeup gone. Eyes crazed with veins.

"Can you see all right?" I said.

He flashed me the finger. "Can you?"

Each girl peeled a long strip of skin from an apple. Diane threw her peel over her shoulder. It fell into an S-shape on the floor.

"S!" Mrs. Powell shouted. "Your husband's initial will be S!"

I sidled up to Paula. There was a smudge of color on her lower lip. Midnight Mauve.

I froze. She flung her peel.

J.

I glanced at Jack. His eyes were fixed on Paula. Paula clutched my shoulder, blushed.

"Oh my God," she said, "I can't believe it, it's a—"

"It's not!" I said. "It's a squiggle! It's just a squiggle!" I kicked the peel. Now it was a squiggle.

Nobody spoke.

I stomped upstairs, burst outside, sat on the curb at the end of the drive. Leaves shocked on lawns. Apples pulped on the pavement.

Jack hunkered down beside me. "What the hell is going on?" he said.

"Don't act all innocent!" I said. "I know what you and Paula were doing in the bathroom!"

"I just kissed her!" he said. "She's cute. We were sitting there. I just kissed her."

I jumped up and bolted. Jack-o'-lanterns smashed on the street. A triangle eye. Half a grin. Trees bandaged with toilet tissue.

DEAD MAN'S CURVE

"Dead is Graham Porter, age twenty-two."
I turn up the radio.

* * *

I've only known one dead guy. Jonathan Worth. I sat two rows behind him in Grade 10 Geography. All through class I'd lean sideways and study him. Black hair squared across his neck. Bum wedged between the bars on his chair

One Valentine's Day I tried sending him a carnation. Student Council was selling them to raise money for dances. I paid my dime and the Social Convener gave me an enclosure card.

"Fill out her name and home form," he said.

"Do I have to sign it?"

***

I clear off the table and iron my good clothes. Black suit, black tie, white shirt. A handkerchief I bought at the Sally Ann. It's white with a stencil-blue monogram. *H.D.C.* Whoever that is.

***

Henderson's held Jonathan's wake from 6 to 9 on a Wednesday evening. I showed up with ten minutes to go. The coat rack half empty. Mr. Henderson sat at a desk beside it.

"Would you care to make a donation?" he said. He passed me a pocket Bible. It had a red cover with gold lettering.

I gave him two bits.

"God bless," he said nudging the register at me. I signed it, *"Friend of the Deceased."*

***

I hang up my ironing and then dash downstreet. The sun's history, the temperature's plunging. I peer into Henderson's but nothing moves. A *COME AGAIN* sign hanging on the door.

At Jaye's I buy an *Examiner*. Graham Porter's front-page.

"Plowed his snowmobile into barbed wire," Mr. Jaye says. "Clotheslined him."

Three wrinkled eggs and a bottle of Jack Daniel's in my fridge. I pour myself a shot, then open the paper to Graham's obituary.

I tear out his photo. He's wearing a graduation robe. Knees at 3 o'clock, chest at noon, head up and out.

I file him in my Bible with the other guys. One electrocuted, two shot, two drowned. One guy had a heart attack.

* * *

Jonathan fishtailed trying to merge off the highway. The car hit a Hydro box. His head pierced the windshield. Mr. Henderson tweezed every shard of glass from his face. He disguised the scars with base. I rubbed a little of it off at the wake.

"Shit." I spun around. The room was empty save

for an old couple on a loveseat. They nodded. I turned back. I stroked Jonathan's fingers and lips and the birthmark beneath his left eyebrow. My groin flush against the casket. Mouth dry as dust.

VICTOR MATURE

Hugh pulled me to the ground and kissed me. Lips, nipples, navel. He yanked off my jeans to continue.

He swallowed, then straddled up my chest. Gripping my ears he fucked my mouth, yodelling like Gene Autry when he came.

An Angus bull answered back. It snorted and hoofed dirt about a hundred yards away.

"We got ourselves an audience!" Hugh said, still holding my ears.

"Jesus Christ," I said. I fumbled backward, boxers around my knees, belt buckle rattling. "It's okay it's okay," I whispered to the cow.

Suddenly Hugh screamed "Soo-eee!" and high-tailed it past me.

The bull moaned and charged.

Hugh hurdled the fence and collapsed laughing. I vaulted over. My left ankle landed sideways on a chunk of cement.

***

In Emergency a nurse stripped me and threaded my arms through a hospital gown. She shot morphine in my butt. My ankle stopped screaming. My head started humming.

A man breezed in and picked up my chart. "I'm Dr. Ogilvie," he said. "Why don't you tell my what happened?"

"Me and Hugh were fooling around. I think I broke something."

He flipped through forms. "And Hugh is?"

"My pal," I said. Or thought I said. I couldn't be sure. I repeated it louder.

The doctor nodded and neared. Lights in my eyes, wood on my tongue. He rolled me toward the wall and scraped a fingernail down my behind. "What exactly were you boys doing?" he said.

"You know," I chuckled. "Messing around."

He stared down over his bifocals. I checked beneath me. Soil and hayseed matted on the white paper sheet.

"Be honest son," he said. "Were you with a girl?"

I said, "Why would I want a girl?"

Snapping on rubber gloves he combed through my pubic hair. Next he squeezed my testicles and pinched my penis.

"Actually that's working pretty good," I said.

* * *

When my folks got there I told them I'd been exploring the old cement works. "I fell through a landing," I said. "Took a half hour to drag myself to the road."

The doctor told them I was stable physically but troubled mentally. "There are things your son confided," he said. He promised to send a summary to our GP.

* * *

Hugh shinned up the drainpipe to the overhang outside my room. I rolled out of bed to meet him.

"You okay?" he said.

"Well I've got a hundred pounds of plaster on my foot."

He pressed his palm against the screen, trapping

no-see-ums underneath. "I'm sorry," he said. He stuck out his lower lip. I let him crawl inside. He tipped me onto the mattress.

"Listen a sec," I said.

He fell on top of me, nibbled at my nose.

"Hugh, the doctor knows."

He froze.

I shoved him off me. "What are we going to do?"

"There's nothing we can do, is there?"

I turned away, my alarm clock tsking from my dresser, Dad sawing logs down the hall.

* * *

I started tacking Rita Hayworth photos over my desk. I took the girly playing cards from Dad's sock drawer and stashed them underneath my pillow for Mom to find.

And I got a girlfriend. Lori Kelly. First day of school she volunteered to help me between classes. Carrying my books, holding my crutches.

After a week I invited her over for a thank-you supper. Mom laid out her bone china. Wine glasses for the adults, juice glasses for the two of us.

* * *

I took Lori to a show. Thugs knocked down Victor Mature. Victor Mature scrambled up, blood rilling out his nose. Derricks pumping crude behind him.

Lori webbed my hand through hers.

There was a whoop from somewhere behind us. I spun around but saw nothing. The picture flickering in people's eyeglasses.

"I'll be right back," I said.

I hobbled to the aisle and headed for the men's room. White lights, white porcelain, white tile. Shoe prints like dance steps on the floor.

Hugh was smoking by the urinals. He stepped forward and gripped my shoulder. His other hand went down my spine.

I pulled back, stumbled, hit the hand dryer.

A toilet flushed. A sliding bolt. A man emerged from a stall and peered over at us.

Hugh wiped his lips with his sleeve. "Evenin'," he said.

The man shot us a backward glance on his way out.

"Good going," I said.

Hugh pulled me close. His eyelashes tickled mine. He said, "This is how much I care."

A burning barn. Chickens flying helter-skelter, horses bucking against smoke. With a wet blanket draped over his head Victor Mature ran into the blaze. I slipped into my seat, hairs coiled on my tongue, pants damp against my thighs.

"Are you okay?" Lori said.

I nodded. "Fine," I said. "What's happening?"

She touched my wrist. Victor Mature's family was cheering, cheeks smeared with grime, ashes snowing down around.

STARGAZE

From Peterborough I took the Greyhound. I checked into Toronto General Hospital. My room was a bed, a chair, a closet. A barred window. Streetcars sparked past in the night.

* * *

First thing in the morning I was sitting in Dr. Vine's office.

"Age?" he said.

"Eighteen," I said. "Sir."

He scribbled on my chart. "How long have you been aware of your inversion?"

I breathed deep. "Eighteen years."

In the examining room I stripped and stretched out on a gurney. He girded my shins and arms, rolled an electric generator up to me. Taped electrodes to my penis and scrotum.

He said, "I'd like you to describe your fantasies involving men."

I shut my eyes. I spoke about kissing Gary Cooper's lips and nipples and stomach and—

Dr. Vine shocked me.

Back in my room I cupped my balls in my palm. Legs cramped. After a couple hours I signed out at the nurses' station and went down to the street.

The July sun. I shuffled north, past Queen's Park and Victoria University. At the Royal Ontario Museum I bought a ticket and wandered into an auditorium where people sat in dentist chairs under a plaster dome. The usher seated me as the house lights died.

Over loudspeakers: *"Welcome to the Milky Way."*

Constellations brightened overhead—the Pleiades, Cepheus, Andromeda—

The auditorium seemed to spin. I gasped.

* * *

Come morning Dr. Vine strapped me down and hooked me up and showed me photographs of naked hulks with brush-cuts flexing their biceps.

I glanced from them to him. He was drumming

his fingertips against the pictures, nails yellow, uncut. My penis limp.

"You're not concentrating," he said. He lined the pictures up on an easel. He ripped the electrodes off my privates and pressed them to my temples.

I blacked out.

* * *

I walked to the planetarium. Sat near the projector. It was dumbbell-shaped, fifteen feet long. Lying lengthwise it projected the night skies of the northern and southern hemispheres. Then it tilted. At a twenty-degree angle it shot out images of the planets. It tilted again and suddenly the sun filled the dome.

* * *

In the morning in Dr. Vine's office. I took off my clothes.

"You're extremely tense," he said. "Can you tell me why?"

"Because you really hurt me yesterday," I said.

"You're generalizing." He wheeled the generator

closer. He wired my temples. "Your behavior," he said. "Your behavior is what hurts. Isn't that so?"

"Yes but I'm not sure—"

He ordered me to think men. Nude men.

"I can't, I'm too nervous."

"Close your eyes *now!*"

* * *

I came to in my room, my pillow bloody. I'd bitten my tongue.

At the Greyhound depot I bought popsicles. My lips were grape when I pulled into Peterborough.

I tramped home to bed. Clouds blanking out the stars.

* * *

Didn't catch a wink till dawn. My alarm went off and I ignored it. Sometime after noon the telephone rang. I picked it up.

It was Dr. Vine. "Admitting told me you'd checked out," he said.

My legs cramped.

"I'm expecting you bright and early tomorrow."

"No it's okay," I stammered. "I think I'm cured."

"If you're not here in the morning I'll be forced to contact your parents. Or the police."

I threw on some clothes and dashed downstreet. The bookstore had nothing. Likewise Hampton's Novelty Shop. At Turnbull's Department Store I snatched up a celestial map and a copy of *The Amateur Astronomer's Guide*.

"You been to the Ex?" the saleslady said. She showed me a flyer for the Peterborough Exhibition. Listed among the attractions—*"Science Fair and Planetarium."*

I hopped the next bus to the fairgrounds. I tore into the Recreation Center. Representing Science were an ant farm and a model of Peterborough's hydraulic liftlock. A papier-mâché sun dangled from a ceiling fan. Nine styrofoam orbs twirled around it.

The solar system.

"That's it?" I said punching my hip. "That's it?" I trudged out into the midway. Wall-to-wall people. Kids swarming the Haunted House, the Caterpillar, the Chairplane. The moon a fingernail clipping.

I staggered up against a cotton candy stand and

shut my eyes. When I opened them I saw a dumbbell tilting in midair. It was cherry red, studded with lights. Instead of weights it had cages full of screaming people.

I fell onto my back, hands pillowing my head, heavenly bodies whirring across the sky.

EX

I started work at the Ex. I put up a fence around the petting zoo. I helped assemble game booths. The Funhouse came in one piece. They lifted it off the truck and plugged it in.

Mom's deep into gardening. Yesterday she tied stuffed animals to stakes and planted them around her vegetables.

* * *

My car's been acting up. The fan belt snapped and I replaced it with a pair of Mom's nylons. Next day the oil pan went.

Tonight I sold ride coupons. Didn't make it home till midnight. Dad worried my car had broken down. He lit a hundred citronella candles and waited on the stoop.

* * *

I drove Dad to Stuart Motors. He chose a camper. Apart from some rust on the axle it's in pretty decent shape. He and Mr. Johnson are going to take it on their trip.

We hitched it to the car. When we got home Mom stood in the driveway and watched us park. Dad got out. Mom stormed away.

At quarter to 4 I left for the fairgrounds. I came home to a dark house. The camper full of shadows. As I drove past it Dad waved. Then he blew out the candles.

* * *

For supper I ate candy apples, caramel corn, cotton candy. I helped folks onto the Zipper. The Zipper's like a Ferris wheel with cages that spin upside down. All night I got pelted with coins and car keys. My gut aching.

* * *

In '49 Dad and Mr. Johnson travelled to Algonquin Park. In '50 they went to the Finger Lakes. Last summer it was the Appalachian mountains in Kentucky. You should see the photos. Hundred-foot gorges. Dad and Mr. Johnson skunked, arms around each other. Pup tent flapping in the wind.

* * *

No word from Dad. Mom visited me at work. We strolled through the Memorial Center. All the prize flowers are wilted, the veggies dried-up. Blue-ribbon baking locked in the scorekeeper's cage.

I won two stuffed animals for Mom's garden.

* * *

Today they tore it down. The Jolly Caterpillar, the Salt-'n-PepperShaker, the Heartbreak Express. When the Conklin trucks had gone I swept the fairgrounds.

I got home at 11. The phone rang. When I picked it up the line was dead. Mom was on the stairs.

"Go to bed," I said.

She just stared at me. She gathered the collar of her nightgown into a fist and held it there.

* * *

Mom's cornflowers are blooming. She gave me one to send you. I crushed it in a dictionary. Hope it gets there okay.

HARDWOOD

Rick picked me up at the cottage at sundown. We sped out onto the highway.

He was wearing jeans. Stroking my thigh I said, "Will linen pants be warm enough?"

"Here's the deal," he said. "You don't talk to me, I won't kill you."

Hayfields, churches, barns. By and by he pulled over by an insulbrick house. He said, "Get in back."

I did. A girl scurried up the drive. She was wearing denim too. She climbed in front and kissed Rick and we were off. Bog, pines, bog ...

She twisted around. "You're Derek? Hi, I'm Kathy. How do you know Rick?"

Rick answered. "His parents' place is next to ours. Mom made me bring him."

She squinted and smiled. "It'll be fun," she said. "Do you have a girlfriend?"

"I have no time for romance," I said. "In Toronto there's always so much to do. The theater, ballet."

Rick grumbled and gunned through a town called Glen Alda. A Shell station and a sand dome. Two bulldozers dozing in the fairground.

"Did you get to the fair this year?" Kathy said. "We had great weather for it."

"I hate carnivals," I said. "They're so tawdry. Do you know what the CNE is?"

"Well I've never actually been . . ."

"Don't bother," I said. "The International Pavilion's the only thing worth seeing. Last year I bought sabots there. You know those wooden shoes Dutch people wear? Well they're *very* comfortable."

She massaged her nape. "Really?" she said. "I guess you know a lot about that stuff."

"I always get A's in Geography," I said.

We turned down a dirt road and crossed a meadow, parked with a half-dozen other cars at the base of a knoll. She grabbed blankets from the trunk. He fished a Mason jar out from under his seat.

"What's that?" I said.

"Know what whiskey is?" he said.

I followed them over the knoll to a falling field. They made for a bunch of kids circling a bonfire. I crouched nearby. Weeds and tallgrass shivering in the breeze.

I counted eighteen people. Two by two they started drifting into the field. Rick and Kathy vanished. A gang of newcomers arrived. One guy mingled his way around the blaze, swigging a beer. Bermuda shorts, baseball cap. Muscles.

I stared till he noticed me.

"Don't believe I know you," he said. He walked over and we shook. His name was Les. He asked who I'd come with and I told him.

"Oh yeah?" he said. "What'd they do, take off with your booze?"

"No no," I said. "I hate alcohol. It kills brain cells."

"What's that supposed to mean?" he said. He spat at my feet and then swaggered toward the fire.

"Les, wait, I—"

Over his shoulder he flipped me the finger.

I rose and dusted my trousers and waded into the field. Burs on my socks. Mosquitoes bleeding my ankles. "Kathy?" I said. "Rick?"

I kicked Rick. In the ribs. He moaned, leapt up, a tepee of Y-front poking out of his fly.

"Get the fuck outta here!" he said.

Kathy flipped onto her stomach, her brassiere like a caterpillar tent in the grass.

"Oh God." I said, "I'm sorry, I didn't know you were—"

"Git before I bust your fucking head!" he said.

I ran back to my patch by the fire. Now we were seven. I waved to Les. He whispered to a buddy. After a minute they rose and walked west into a thicket. They emerged clutching lumber. While they fed the flames I investigated.

Roots veined the trail. I crept forward, steadying myself on branches. Finally I came on a shack in a clearing. Two of its walls had been stripped away. On the ground lay a heap of tobacco tins and newspapers. Two-by-fours.

Tottering down the trail with two boards on my shoulder, two under my arm. I dropped them by the fire. Mouse turds on my clothes. Glasses streaked with sweat. I dried them off but Les had gone. Everyone had. Belches and giggles floating on the air.

I heaved a board into the fire.

The next board I heaved slid across the mound. Embers scattered into the tallgrass. The tallgrass took.

"Hey you guys!" I said.

Flames jumping blade to blade, weeds curling into red-hot filaments.

"Guys?" I said.

I dashed up the knoll. The blaze was burning in a V across the field. Smoke where trees should've been.

Far off someone shouted, "Fire!" Suddenly the smoke was full of shadows running and howling. Les loomed up and vanished. I bolted to the car. The keys were in it. I gunned up to the edge of the highway. A wall of pines one direction, same thing the other. A porcupine smeared on the dividing line.

BUOY

Bryan Benson did a cartwheel and a flip, then walked on his hands. The class clapped.

Coach called me up next. I crouched at the edge of the mat. I somersaulted. I somersaulted again. Then with a quarter-turn to the right I somersaulted twice more and stood, arms outspread. Spine paining.

"Whaddya call that?" Bryan said.

The guys laughed. Coach walked up to me. Pointing to my neck he said: "What's that rash?"

* * *

Two weeks previous it had been a pimple. Then it had multiplied into a half-dozen nickel-sized blotches. The blotches became scales. When Coach saw them he phoned my mom. Mom drove me to Peterborough that afternoon. A doctor at Nicholl's

Hospital pricked my back with needles. He drew blood till my elbows were blue as blackberries.

* * *

With lupus the body's immune system attacks itself. The doctor admitted me and dosed me with penicillin twice a day. He kept my drapes drawn, to shield me from sunlight. And he injected me full of a steroid called hydrocortisone.

Word ripped through Nephton. My minister brought me a bottle of chlorophyll water. Schoolteachers brought me chocolates. The Bensons visited once.

My body slathered in butter, wrapped in Saran.

Mrs. Benson smiled. "You're looking well."

Bryan snickered.

Mrs. Benson said, "Bryan got a job at Hiller's Marina for the summer."

"That's swell," I whispered.

* * *

During exam week I lay with ice packs on my

knee and elbow joints. I celebrated my birthday by peeing into cups. At supper the nurses brought me a cupcake decorated with the number sixteen.

Then the blotches began to vanish. Just like that. By week's end my bones had stopped aching. My doctor said: "It'll be like this as long as you live. Flare and remit. Flare and remit."

Mom and Dad drove me home. Trees flowering. Buttercups on scrub land. "I think a celebration's in order," Dad said, turning down Stoney Lake Road toward Hiller's Marina.

The lunchroom faced the lake. It was packed. The Reynolds, the Tuckers, the Greens—folks kept stopping by the table to ask how I felt. I smiled and nodded, eyeing the mirror on the wall. My bald crown. Sunken cheeks.

"Excuse me a sec," I said.

Grabbing a washroom key I stepped out onto the deck. A bunch of guys were sitting out there. Bryan included.

"Check out the bone rack," he said. "Hey, how about a somersault?"

* * *

Come morning I hatched a Charles Atlas regimen. In my bedroom I did sit-ups, push-ups, stretches. When I told Mom I was going for a walk she said: "Honey, the sun."

My face slicked with petroleum jelly I took a walk through the bush behind the house. A couple hundred yards that first day, a couple hundred more the next. I skirted the nepheline syenite mine. I came on abandoned shafts flooded with greenish water, signs nailed to trees—*CAUTION: NO SHALLOW AREA.* I followed the train tracks of long-gone lumber camps.

After a couple weeks I made it to Stoney Lake.

* * *

In the morning I put trunks on under my trousers and told Mom I'd be gone awhile. At Stoney Lake I stripped down and waded in. I did a breaststroke at first, coaxing myself, *breathe, stroke, breathe, stroke.* I passed cottages, waves gurgled around docks. When my arms cramped I did the egg-beater with my legs. When my legs cramped I backstroked. When I cramped head to toe I treaded water.

Took me an hour to get there. I dragged myself onto the dock, gulping air. There were men sitting at picnic tables, filleting fish on newspaper. I staggered past, into the marina. Cold rippled from a fridge full of Coke. It soothed my sunburnt shoulders and neck.

"Bryan here?" I said.

I collapsed to the floor.

Two men carried me out to the side stoop and lay me on a bench. One fanned me. He said: "You want me to find Bryan?"

I moaned and forced myself up onto my elbow. I tried to focus. Kids were winging softballs around. Minnows racing around bait shop bathtubs.

LOVE LIES DEEP

The man stalked down Seasonal and stashed a tin of shortbreads in his coat. I pursued him out the Simcoe St. exit.

"Excuse me sir," I said tapping his shoulder. "I work at Turnbull's and—"

Boom. He coldcocked me. I came to on the sidewalk.

When I got home I crushed ice for a compress. Uncle Trevor padded downstairs in pajamas, cowlick standing on end.

"Long day huh?" he said.

"Yep."

"The other guy look as bad?"

"Yep."

He scooped a palmful of the ice into a tumbler. "Your problem is you're too scrawny. You should bulk up." He pushed up a sleeve and flexed his arm.

"That's a hundred push-ups every morning."

"Congratulations." I crossed into the family room and flicked the radio on. Bing Crosby.

I sank onto the sofa. Trevor appeared in the doorway, sipping a whiskey highball.

"Carol and I are heading downtown first thing," he said. "If you'd like to join us."

"Maybe."

He eased down beside me. Sweeping aside the compress he fingered my eyebrow.

I kissed his chin. I kissed his mouth and slid my hand under his top. Up to his nipple, down his treasure trail, past the knotted drawstring of his bottoms . . .

He gripped my wrist. "Sorry pal. I've already had it tonight."

"Well go for the record," I whispered.

"Good idea." He stood and shook off my hand. "I'll go see if Carol's up to it."

"I was joking," I said. "Just sit down."

I grabbed at his leg. He dodged me, then sauntered to the staircase in the hall. Highball sloshing.

"You be a good boy," he said, "and we'll see what Santa brings."

"Fuck you."

He smirked and disappeared upstairs. Bing crackling on the radio.

I shut him off and turned in.

***

The sky spat all next morning. Trevor let Carol off at Market Hall. I volunteered to go with her.

"Thanks hon," she said, "but I was hoping you'd take him for a shave."

"Aw she loves it," he said winking at me and scratching the shadow on his chin.

Straight razor, lavender foam. He tipped the barber a buck and we walked toward Turnbull's, navigating slush puddles and sandwich boards and Santas from the Sally Ann.

He said, "What do you think Carol'd like for Christmas?"

"How should I know?" I said.

I tailed him through the perfume and jewelry departments. In Women's Wear he picked up a floral housedress.

"No no no," I said. "Try a nice bathrobe. Or slippers."

"You try it," he said. "I need coffee."

* * *

Trevor and Carol gave me an electric razor. "What is it?" he kept asking as I unwrapped it. He gave her a silk blouse and a White Shoulders bath assortment. Thirty percent off with my discount.

"Trevor they're perfect," Carol said.

* * *

The house shifting under frost. The groaning staircase. Trevor stole into the room and crawled up my bed. He reeked of whiskey.

"Hey," he said.

I turned away. "Fuck off," I said.

He squeezed my leg. "Where's your Christmas spirit?" he said and kissed the back of my neck.

I rolled over and unbuttoned his pajamas. While I blew him I fingered his asshole. That way his smell stayed with me for days.

He came, then jerked me off.

I scurried to the bathroom, returning on tiptoe with tissues. "Want one?" I said.

My window rattled. Across the field lights blinked in an upside-down V.

"Trevor," I said. "Trevor wake up," I said. I eased down beside him. I kissed his throat. Then I started sucking it, busting veins, a bruise the shape of my mouth blooming beneath his skin.

HANDS

This year Kelly asked her parents to send her to the world trapshooting championship in Vandalia, Ohio. The Grand American Handicap, it's called.

"I can take the bus," she said. "It'll hardly cost anything."

Mrs. Forrest said, "Honey, I'm not sure trapshooting's the sort of sport you should be involved in."

She clamped her hands on her hips. "Oh really?" she said. "And what is?"

Mrs. Forrest suggested ballet.

* * *

Kelly drove to my house and we walked downtown. Dandelions bursting from cracks in the cement.

"I can give you twenty bucks," I said.

She smiled, punched my arm. We stopped in at every store on George St. Silver's Shoes and Walkwel's both needed summer help. On the street she told me she'd rather die than touch people's feet.

"Anyway," she added, "my folks would find me at Walkwel's."

We wandered up to the clock tower and south on Charlotte, ducking into Hampton's Novelty to buy Marlboros. Kelly asked Mr. Hampton if he had anything available.

"What do you know about gags?" he said.

"What do you wanna know?"

He folded his arms. "I don't pay much."

"Then I won't strain myself."

He hired her part-time.

* * *

Mr. Hampton kept a candy counter crammed with Hands fireworks. Bombardos, maroons, mines. Kelly discovered a false bottom in a drawer of Burning Schoolhouses. Hidden below were packets of powder. *RED SPARKS, BLUE SPARKS, GOLD TWINKLES.*

"What are these for?" she said.
"Mind your own business," he said.

***

Kelly dumped a bag of fireworks on my deck. She pulled a jackknife out of her pocket, slit a Roman candle and sliced away the wrapping. Eight aggie-sized balls on a bed of black powder. "Stars," she said. "They flare in midair." Next she slit a Fountain. Same kind of casing but a half-inch wider nozzle. "Just like a gun," she said. "The fuller the choke the farther the stuff flies."

***

Next weekend she brought over twenty batons wrapped in kraft. "Paper towel tubes," she said running her fingers over a baton. "The powder's from Dad's shells."

We wrapped them in white tissue and brainstormed names. She liked "Stiff Shooters" and "Exploding Parents." I painted the names onto the shafts in gold.

Grab Bag

* * *

I parked on the shoulder of the highway, propped our *HOMEMADE FIREWORKS* sign against the trunk. A half-mile south Kelly lit a Fountain. A gold zipper against the denim-colored sky. Cars slowed to look. By the time she'd jogged down to meet me I'd sold out of stock.

* * *

Dip wires in shellac and steel filings. *Presto!*—sparklers. Kelly sealed them in sandwich bags, four to a pack.

We launched them near the swimming hole on River Road. She held a Stiff Shooter in her hands, blasted stars at passing boats.

A car with Ohio plates pulled over. Two guys in shorts and T-shirts stepped out. "Your friend's crazy," one guy said.

"Do you guys know where Vandalia is?" I said.

They asked why and I motioned to Kelly. She was loping toward us, hair blackened where she tucks it behind her ears.

"You a trapshooter?" shouted one guy.

"I used to be," she said. "Now I'm a pyrotechnician!"

She copied the addresses of motels and restaurants in Vandalia. She asked the guys for their phone numbers.

"You gonna tell your parents?" I said.

"I'll mail them a postcard when I get there," she said.

* * *

Dominion Day I posted myself in a turnaround between Bridgenorth and Lakefield. She stood by a *PLEASE DON'T LITTER* sign, trying to light a candle. Twice the breeze blew out her Zippo. Finally the quickmatch caught.

So did her sweatshirt. She tumbled to the gravel. I screamed. The candle whistled onto the road and *bang!*—copper blazed blue, cryolite and barium chlorate fused into purple, charcoal exploded in gold streamers. The blacktop melting beneath.

I found her in a ditch, submerged up to her face in dead water. The ambulance guys told me they'd contact her parents. A policeman jotted down my name and address.

"Don't go far," he said.

CATTLE CALL

Eric brought me a cowboy shirt to wear. It was black with white stitching and snaps instead of buttons.

Uncle Jamie stopped me on my way out the door. "You know the rules," he said. "No alcohol. Play today pay tomorrow."

The water tank atop Quaker Oats was floodlit. Ditto city hall and the courthouse.

"Here's my place." Eric cruised by a redbrick building. The Red Dog Hotel. "Not bad huh?"

We blew through Peterborough and in no time we'd arrived. He parked by a dumpster. He checked his hair in the rearview.

Tex Ritter singing "Blood on the Saddle." Wood shavings on the floor. While he went for beers I grabbed a booth. Half standing I scoped around. There were a few leaning on the bar, a few two-stepping with boyfriends. A doll in a scoop top by the juke.

Eric came back with a girl. "This here's Mr. Walter's nephew," he said. "I'm showing him the ropes this summer."

"Yeah?" She tapped a smoke against her pack. Orange nails.

We washed the beer down with whiskey. I held it all in till my dick was piss-hard. Teetering at the urinal with one arm bracing the wall, a flystrip twirling overhead. Eric fumbled with my hind pocket.

"Here's the keys," he said. "Ask her for a walk."

She said sure. Trying to keep a poker face I snaked behind her through the crowd. Eric and two strangers were hallooing me and flashing thumbs up from a different booth. I turned and flipped them the bird just before passing outside.

"Nice night eh?" I said.

"Real nice," she said. "Wanna sit in the pickup?"

We locked the doors and cranked the windows up. She moved close.

"You smell beautiful," I said.

She laughed and stroked me from knee to thigh.

My throat gurgled. When she kissed me it gurgled again.

"Sorry I—"

"It's all right." She tongued my lips and we frenched. A flick of her hand undid my belt. My zipper. She hunched and husked my shorts and my dick curled out, come gummed at the tip.

"Is it okay?" I said.

"Sshh." She choked it down. After a couple swallows the suction was strong enough. Bang.

Between gasps I thanked her.

"No problem," she said adjusting her bobby pins.

* * *

Around 4 I snuck to the bathroom and beat off. I still had blue balls come daybreak. The buffalo bawling and rumbling in off the western fields. Jamie was dropping hay bales and salt licks from the flatbed. I tucked in my sheets and bounded downstairs to the kitchen.

Saturdays forenoon Jamie and Dar peddle meat in town at Market Hall. After breakfast I helped pack coolers and went with them. We set up in a stall by the Charlotte St. entrance. On the counter we displayed a buffalo doll and a placard picturing which cuts come from which parts of the animal. Round and loin and rump roasts sold out first. When business died off Jamie let me go.

I wandered the aisles sampling freebies, maple fudge and peaches and curds. One farmer had a daughter my age working. I lined up in front of her.

"One cuke please," I said.

"One?"

"Yep." I stared at her lips, the freckles on her nose.

She smiled and shrugged and passed me my purchase. "Five cents."

I gave her a quarter. "Keep the change."

Candy carts and souvenir stands dotted Market Square. I bought a postcard of George St. *"Dear Mom and Dad sorry I haven't written blah blah blah."* I walked to Jaye's Variety for a stamp. Two bobbysoxers were scarfing down Jujubes outside.

"Hi there," I said.

"Do I know you?" said one girl. A redhead. Built.

"I'm Derek."

"And I'm Lily-Jo-Mae."

Her friend giggled and scraped her sandal along the cement.

"Fresh off the farm?" said red.

I hid the cucumber behind my back.

* * *

We topped up our thermoses and took off through the stock gate into the compound. Clay then chess then scrub. The buffalo were clustered to the east, scratching themselves against silver birches. Scrolls of bark clung to their fur.

Spring runoff had stripped and gullied topsoil. Fence posts across the northern boundary had tipped. Eric and I righted them, tamped soil around the bases. Shirts stuffed in our waistbands, skin scorching. The tattoo on his arm faded to the green color of his pants.

* * *

Coyotes cried through the night. Dogs and birds answering back. I was up at dawn. Jamie filled the feed bins and we waited. Bulls appeared first, two tons apiece including horns. None missing. Next came cows trailed by their young. As he counted calves his face fell.

"You lads keep an eye out," he said. "And take traps."

I dug some number four-and-a-halfs out of the shed. After lubing them with lard I bagged them in burlap sacks padded with spruce and balsam twigs. Eric arrived and I told him what Jamie'd said.

"Figured that." He loaded the flatbed and climbed behind the wheel. We drove in silence toward the woods that stretched beyond the ranch's northern boundary. He flipped his visor and a pouch of Red Man tumbled to his lap. He offered me a plug. I accepted.

He downshifted. "Lookit."

Three blobs cropped out of the hardscrabble. Two were turkey buzzards. They eyed us, then turned and spread their wings and labored skyward.

He parked and we hopped out.

"Jesus." I pinched my nose. The calf was a shell of fur and bone and blackflies. Stringy guts webbed the ground.

He kicked at a hoof. "Might as well set friggin'

mousetraps. What we need's poison. Poison meat. The mother'd eat it and puke it up for the cubs and then they'd all die."

He hawked his chaw.

* * *

I lit out toward town then hung a right at Brealey Dr. but nothing seemed familiar. I turned down a county road and the asphalt tapered into a single dirt lane. A man was torching tent caterpillars that had nested in roadside trees. I asked for directions and he sketched a map in the sand.

At Benny's two drunks were duking it out on the dance floor. The bouncer waited ringside, baseball bat in hand. I scouted around for Eric. Five or six bodies were sardined into each booth. I spotted two guys I remembered meeting. Or seeing.

"Hey," I said. "You seen Eric Beech?"

"Who wants to know?" one of them said.

"I'm the guy from the other night, the one with the lady."

"Oh, the one with the *lady*. Now I recognize you." He patted the plank beside him.

I sat.

"I'm Dwight, this is Reg."

"Good to know you," I said.

"You're sure dressed to kill."

"What're you drinking?" said Reg.

"Anything," I said, "if someone'll get it for me."

I gave him a sawbuck and he bought a tray of shooters. We shotgunned them all. Ditto round two.

Dwight tipped a glass against my lips. "Bottoms up cowboy."

"Had enough." I boxed air and tried to stand but the booze rushed my brain. One foot caught the table post and I tumbled from the booth. Catcalls and applause from the crowd. Dwight and Reg shouldered me to the lot. I said, "I think you better take me home."

They were already rooting through my pockets for keys.

Curled up in the backseat, clothes battered in sawdust and sweat. One of the guys uncapped a mickey and the fumes flooded my nostrils. Vomit lumped in my throat. I heard radio, the turn signal, gravel under the tires. When I tried to say stop I retched again. Finally Dwight braked. I scrambled out and puked twice on the same patch of bluebells.

I rolled over to find them emptying the trunk. Jugs of washer fluid, Dar's mackinaw, tire chains arced through the air. I bent my legs to rise. Reg knocked me back.

"Not yet cowboy," he said.

Save for far-off forks of lightning everything beyond the headlights was dark. A ridge of spiky treetops. Dwight uncovered a crowbar and carried it over.

"Take off your clothes."

I teared. "What are you gonna do?"

He whacked my arm. "Shut up and give them."

I worked my right boot off. Then my left.

Reg crouched and popped open my shirt. Next he unbuttoned my jeans and yanked them off. My shorts came off too. "Lift your feet," he said.

I cupped my dick.

He squinted at me a sec. "You little fucker . . ."

I flipped over and jackknifed my legs to sprint. A boot stamped me to the ground.

"You calling us fags? You calling us fags?"

The tip of the crowbar struck my tailbone. I gasped and writhed and shielded my rear with my hands. Dwight kicked them away.

"You want it up the ass?" He jabbed there and missed. He jabbed again.

I pressed fingers to my hole and they came up slick and black.

The car roared off in a squall of dust and pebbles. I weaved toward the taillights, sobbing, guts aflame.

Somewhere something howled. I howled back.

THE HISTORY OF COUNTRY MUSIC

"The band needs trombones," said Steve, the Class President.

"The band needs talent," said me. I sat in back.

He ignored me. "The Lions needs jerseys. And the Chess Club needs boards. So Student Council has decided to hold a Halloween Carnival, to raise funds. They've asked us to organize the pumpkin carving contest."

"Goody-goody," I said.

"I've divided you into committees based on your skills." He gave Publicity to the arty kids. Rich kids got Prizes. Sports got Clean-up. "Did I forget anyone?"

My arm shot up.

"You don't have any skills," he said. "Except being rude."

***

The old lady led me to her backyard. Pie plates clanging on stakes. To scare crows.

"If you donate a pumpkin," I said, "our Baking Committee will be happy to make it into a delicious pumpkin pie for you to eat after the carnival."

She signed the sign-up sheet. I cut one off the vine, put it in my wheelbarrow. The lady at the next house gave me two. She had lots. Her scarecrow was a suit stuffed with straw.

My load got tippy. I started out toward the school. Then turned. Tore off my nametag. Tossed the sign-up sheet. Dumped my haul behind my outhouse. Some were heirlooms. My scarecrow was a post with strings nailed to it. Tied to the strings were crows. They were barely flapping. Too tired to caw.

"Caw!" I said.

***

I carved triangle eyes. Triangle nose. Mouth like cogwheels coming together.

Not a bit scary. I tossed it. When it hit the ground the face caved in. Now it looked scary.

The contest was: The scariest jack-o'-lantern wins. I tried everything. On my practice pile I had pumpkins with one eye. Three eyes. Fangs. Squirrels like smoke inside.

I pulled up a fresh one. Gutted it. Gave it little round eyes. Like Steve's. I traced his nose with the tip of the knife. Slashed out two big nostrils. Like Steve's.

I carved a round mouth. Stuck a finger in to smooth it. Then unzipped my fly.

It was a little tight. I knifed it again. The knife stuck. When I forced it it warped.

My hand slick with seeds. Slipped. My pinky split open. Skin peeled back over flesh and bone.

I might've passed out.

* * *

Trees the colors of vegetables. I walked to the hospital. It was three miles. By the crow. My hand held up over my head. As if I had a question.

"You get a lot of this this time of year?" I said. "Pumpkin accidents?"

"Actually, you're the first. Ever." The doctor swabbed it, then stitched me up with black thread.

I didn't feel a thing.

"You might have severed a nerve. Maybe a tendon." He mixed plaster of paris and put a cast on me. Elbow to wrist. When it dried he stapled a rubber band to it.

"You've got to exercise the tendon while it's fusing. Or else it'll get brittle." He picked up the other end of the rubber band. Stapled it to my pinky nail.

My hand curled into a claw.

I picked up a scalpel. It fell out of my hand.

"That can be your costume," he said. "The Claw!"

* * *

During the carving contest Steve grabbed my cast. "Too bad," he said. "Can I sign it?"

He signed it: *Derek's a jerk.*

"Next," the Principal said. "The costume contest!"

The carnival was in the gym. Kids piled on a stage. A bum with a silk flower. A ghost in a monogrammed sheet.

Next up—Talent Contest.

A guy from the Drama Club recited Shakespeare. A linebacker lifted weights.

Four girls went up. Their dresses were tissue. They waved flashlights. *"Shine little glow worms,"* they sang. *"Glimmer. Glimmer."*

"I am about to demonstrate the limits of human endurance," said the next guy. He cleared his throat. "My name is Yon Yonson, I come from Wisconsin, I work in the lumber mills there. As I walk down the street, all ask, 'What's your name?' And I tells them 'My name is Yon Yonson, I come from Wisconsin...'"

The crowd booed. I jumped on stage. Grabbed the mike. My rubber band was red. I plucked it. I raised my pinky and the rubber tensed. I plucked it again. Sang: *"What a beautiful thought I am thinking, concerning that Great Speckled Bird..."*

MEN WITH BROKEN HEARTS

THIS WEEKEND—HANK WILLIAMS AND HIS DRIFTING COWBOYS!

I tore the poster off the lamppost, then ran home and taped it to my bedroom wall. I phoned my friend Michael. I begged Dad to lend me money for a ticket.

He offered me a deal. He'd buy tickets for me and Michael. In exchange we'd clean an old hunting camp he'd bought.

"Hunting is so barbaric," I said.

* * *

First thing next morning Michael and I headed north in Dad's truck. Hank bursting through radio static.

"Whaddya think he'll open with?" Michael said.

"'Lovesick Blues.' For sure. That's his signature song."

The driveway teemed with wild oat and pine saplings. It led to a frame cabin in a clearing. We found a two-seater outhouse. A rabbit bobbing in a lidless well.

"This is so disgusting," I said.

He scythed the yard, I swept the cabin. Shotgun shells, mouse turds, newspapers from the '30s. *DEPRESSION CONTINUES, DEPRESSION DEEPENS.* I chucked it all. The linoleum peeling in every corner. A square behind the stove lifted up entirely. I spied a chain hooked to the floor. I yanked it. The floor creaked open.

"Michael!"

He crept down the ladder. I tagged after. The root cellar was about six feet long though it wasn't much wider than his shoulders. Clay walls. Rotten potatoes underfoot.

"What do you think?" he said. "Get a couple girls down here, some candles . . ."

"Are you joking?" I said pinching my nose. "It's *putrid!*"

***

That evening at home I worked on my shirt, a white Stay-Press short-sleeved number. With a pencil I sketched two half-notes over the breast pockets. I smeared glue between the lines and poured a bag of emerald sequins over top.

Dad came in and frowned. I told him that Hank's shirts and blazers had fringed cuffs and yokes, beaded horseshoes and lassos, iron-on guitar decals. One jacket sported the first two bars of "Lovesick Blues," the musical notation in royal piping, the lyrics in aqua rhinestones.

***

The following day Michael and I shingled and painted for eight hours. After dining on baked beans and chicken we unrolled sleeping bags and bedded down on the cabin floor, our transistor blasting.

"*Next,*" said the D.J., "*we'll be cooking something up with Mr. Hank Williams.*"

I whooped and clapped.

"You think he's in town?" Michael said.

"Probably tomorrow."

"Where do you figure he'll stay?"

"Princess Gardens maybe. Maybe the Holiday Inn." I curled up on my side. Smoke coiling off a Pic. On the radio: "Hey Good Lookin'."

Michael kissed my neck.

I sat up like a shot. "What are you doing?"

"I thought maybe . . ."

I gaped at him.

"I'm better looking than Hank."

"You're a fruit!"

"What about you?" he said. "What about your shirt?" He stared at me a moment. Then he got up, put on his jeans and stalked out of the cabin.

"Where are you going? Michael?"

The truck engine drowned me out. I dashed outside. Taillights shrank and died away.

* * *

At daybreak I tramped to the road. Eyelids flagging. A family in a Monarch picked me up. They took me to Jack Lake Marina and I phoned home from there.

Dad came to get me. His cowlick standing on end, pajama top tucked into jeans. We returned to camp. No Michael.

"You've got ten seconds to tell me what the hell is going on," Dad said.

I said I didn't know.

"People just don't pack up and leave! Were you drinking? Was he sneaking off to see some girl?"

* * *

We combed Peterborough. The Victory Grill, the Greeks Restaurant, the lookout up on Armour Hill. On every lamppost a poster—*TONIGHT! DIRECT FROM THE GRAND OLE OPRY! ONE SHOW ONLY!* We drove to Michael's place. I explained to his parents that he'd disappeared during the night.

"But he'll be back by 7," I said. "He won't miss Hank."

They all scowled. Dad said, "You can damn well forget Hank."

The sky was streaked with pink as we set out for home. I flipped the radio on and caught the tail end of "Window Shopping."

Dad flipped it off. "I'm gonna call the cops," he said.

A siren shut him up. By Market Hall he pulled over to let a police cruiser pass. Tailing the cruiser was a Ford Packard with Alabama plates. In the back sat a man in a ten-gallon hat.

I jumped from the car. I raced down Charlotte Street, behind the Bell Building. Half a block from the Brock Ballroom I heard a guitar twang. I snatched a ticket from my wallet. Panting I fought my way through the foyer and across the dance floor and up to the stage. The Drifting Cowboys were tuning, uniformed in black trousers and cowboy shirts. With a one-two-three they launched into the intro to "Lovesick Blues."

Hank stepped from the wings. He was taller than me, skinnier. Hunched up like a bass clef.

My eyes filled. I threw my arms up.

Then he fell. His knees buckled and he flopped onto his guitar. Struggling up he staggered to the mike. "Fuckin' fuckin' fuck," he said. The band repeated the intro. Hank glared offstage. When he fell again he took the mike stand with him. His hat rolled off, a white Stetson, sweatband yellowed.

I reached for it.

"Get away!" A man scooted onstage and grabbed the hat. He went over and lifted Hank by the shoulders. The bassist lifted Hank's feet.

Hank waved.

PASSING ON

Hair is dead protein the body ejects. Chris plucks a strand from his head. It's blond. I take off my glasses and examine it under the microscope.

"Atoms are the basic units of everything. They're so small they're invisible yet they pack enough power to kill." This is what our teacher told us.

Four weeks Grandpa lay in the hospital, lungs turning to pus. Doctors pumped him full of penicillin. Nothing helped.

* * *

I boxed up the things in Grandpa's den. In a cedar chest crammed with papers I discovered a note from his grandmother signed *"L.S. McCormick."*

"When Grandpa was twenty," Dad said, "he

changed the 'i' in his surname to 'a.' He thought it looked less Catholic that way."

* * *

I meet Chris in the school foyer so I can walk into the locker room with him. I change in a stall in the washroom. When I come out he's in his BVDs, brown tufts furring his armpits. Nipples.

* * *

When I was six Grandpa gave me a brush and a razor without a blade so I could pretend to shave. My top lip was the first place I got hair. "It's just peach fuzz," he said. He warned me that once I started shaving my beard would grow out stubbly. That's how my pubic hair came in. One or two strands at a time. I trimmed them every night.

* * *

The undertaker never met Grandpa before he embalmed him. This explains why at his wake

Grandpa's hair was parted on the left side not the right. Otherwise he looked good. Face powdered, lips rouged. Belly full of an astringent that cooked his organs.

* * *

In October our Science teacher takes our class on an overnight field trip. He teaches us tricks for surviving in Nature—how to start a fire without matches, how to build a lean-to out of twigs. Everyone makes a pinbox camera and photographs the woods. I point mine at Chris. He won't stand still for ten minutes. When the picture comes out it's blurry.

* * *

My family formed a receiving line at Grandpa's wake. Before passing the casket folks would shake hands with me and Dad and hug my mom and sister. "What fine looking children," they'd say. And to me: "You look so much like your father."

***

Grandpa phoned my mother at the hospital right after my sister was born. "Good stuff," he said, "but you're going to have to try again." When I was delivered he said, "That's more like it. Keep the McCormack name alive."

***

Campfire songs at 9, marshmallows at 9:30. Boys and girls retire to separate cabins. I change into pajamas in the bathroom. Chris and I flip a quarter for the top bunk. I get bottom.

Just after midnight someone knocks at the window. Chris jumps down and opens it. The other guys are either sleeping or pretending to sleep. I hold my breath. Even when someone steps on my arm climbing into the top bunk, I still hold my breath.

The boards above me begin to creak. Whispers I can't understand. I get out of bed and look. I can see Chris, his arms and shoulders. Her hand on the back of his head.

***

Eons ago one microbe attacked another and engulfed it. Made the other one a part of itself. The result was a new microbe, stronger and with a longer life span. "This," said our teacher, "was the first example of sexual intercourse." Which sheds light on a lot of things. Pneumonia. Gangrene. Atrophy. Putrefy. Corrupt. Different names for the same thing.

***

Chris showed up at Grandpa's wake in suit and tie. I excused myself from the line. We snuck out the back door and sat on the steps. He put his arm around my shoulders. I rested my head against his neck. His aftershave smelled like lilacs. I shivered accidentally.

"It's okay," he whispered. "It's okay."

WISH BOOK
A Catalogue of Stories

THE JOKER

The kid's trying on a fake moustache. I sneak up, shake itching powder down his neck.

He rips off his shirt.

* * *

Some kid blowing his allowance on ink gum, soap biscuits, rubber matches.

I point to my lapel. "Smell my rose."

"You're not squirting me," he says.

* * *

Some kid rifling through fireworks. Victory Dipped Sticks. Golden Shower Torches.

I call him to the counter. Show him girly cards. He shuffles through them, pop-eyed. In his pants—an exploding cigar.

***

I give a kid gum. Red-hot. He spits it out, gasps for air.

I fetch him a drink.

"That a dribble glass?" he says.

"No."

He drinks, wipes his lips. "What's in it?"

"Water."

And knockout drops. The kid teeters, collapses.

I lock the front door. I drag him into the stockroom. Strip him. His chest flat as a pinball board. Bumper nipples. I shave around them. His pits. Pubes. I gather the hair, cut it up fine, funnel it into packets.

Itching powder.

THE JUNIOR BUSINESSMAN

It was a squirrel. "You hold it by the tail," I said. "The front paws hook the oven rack. So you can pull it out when it's hot." It was carved from cedar.

"What's it do that oven mitts can't?" the club leader said. Days he worked at a department store downtown. Nights he supervised our meetings at the school. "And who'd buy it?"

The guys tee-heed. I stalked into the hall and through the first door I saw. Janitor's closet. I stood there.

The leader found me. "Buck up," he said. "Not every product's gonna be a winner."

I hurled the squirrel.

"You gotta move on. Another dream, another scheme. A Junior Businessman's never broke as long as he's rich in ideas."

He left. I palmed my tie flat. My hair. Thought: *Think, think, think.*

When I got back to the gymnasium the club was gone. A man was pushing chairs into a ring. Brown shirt, brown stockings, brown neckerchief. A green plume in his hat.

"You here for Scouts?" he said.

And held up his hand, thumb pinning his pinky down.

* * *

From my haversack I pulled a potholder made of balsam twigs. "Twenty cents," I said.

"Anything cheaper?" the kid said.

A fid whittled from maple. "For splicing knots," I said.

He took it. I cleared away pinecones and needles and displayed stock on the ground. Guys snuck to the glade and bought tent pegs and brushwood brooms. Broilers made of maple twigs. Dish mops: rags stapled to twigs.

"I've gotta start a fire," one kid said.

I sold him a fuzz stick, pine whittled into the

shape of a shaving brush. "Pile kindling around it," I said. "Rub it on a stone."

"Got any maps?" one kid said.

I did, a pencil sketch of the camp—mess tent, bivouacs, johns. A forest of arrows around it. Squiggles were creeks.

He paid a quarter.

Next kid had pennies. I slipped him an ink drawing.

"It's smudged!" he said.

"Pretend they're bogs," I said.

Far off a trumpet squealed. I packed up. Tenderfoots regrouped by the flagpole.

"A Scout must be crafty, inventive, industrious," the Scoutmaster said. "Has each of you completed a badge requirement?"

THE BULLY

"I'm gonna whip your hide!" I said.

The Trailblazer ducked into the woods. He got a fifteen-minute head start. Then the hunt was on.

The Scoutmaster lined us up. "On your marks, get—"

I took off.

* * *

The guy crouched. I crouched. He stared into the sun. I stared into the sun. Saw shadows stuck to grass.

The Trailblazer's footprints.

"I'm on him!" I shouted.

"You're on him?" the guy said.

I knocked him over, ran ahead.

***

"You stupid?" I said. "It's nothing!"

The guy slouched off. I snatched it up—a maple leaf beneath a sumac tree. Further on I found an apple core under ferns. Boot treads on greenrot.

The Trailblazer walking backward across sand, blanking his tracks with a bough.

I sacked him.

***

At the campfire the Scoutmaster promoted us to second-class Scouts.

He awarded me a proficiency badge in Stalking.

"The champ!" I said. Danced a touchdown dance.

***

Snap. A twig woke me. I crawled out of my tent. Doubled my fists. There were three of them.

They saluted me.

"Scout's honor," one guy said. "You can't really track till you know."

"You're gonna teach me?"

They shrugged, filed into bush. I jumped into my boots. A ways from camp they flicked on flashlights. Deerflies zeroed in. The duff smelled like deer.

A clearing. An island of rock. We hopped on. They shone beams at stick drawings.

"This is it?" I said. "Hopscotch?"

"They're in the stone. They're Indian symbols."

Turtle shaped like a stop sign. Snakey squiggles with moss for heads.

"They'd initiate braves," he said. "They'd starve you and smear blood on you and get you drunk and after a couple days a spirit would come and take you over and you'd get all crazy. You'd scratch it into rock and then your souls would be eternally entwined."

A man with the sun for a head. A man with arrows for hands.

"If you're going to be a master tracker," he said, "you can't just follow an animal. You've got to become an animal."

"Baloney," I said.

"We don't let everyone know the secret," he said. "Only a few. The talented ones." He pointed to the other two. "His Indian name's Bear in the Marsh. He's Eagle of Deep Lake. I'm Rabid Wolf."

I stripped buck naked.

"Now dance around. And shout. And think Indian."

I hopped around. Shook my fist like a tomahawk. Beat my chest like a tom-tom.

"Oh great one!" he said. "Send the visions!"

"Oh great one!" I said. "Send the visions!"

"See anything?"

"I dunno," I said, panting. "I might've."

"Keep going."

Head jerking, arms flapping. Stone barked my soles. I dropped down, sucking air, sweating.

"Guess they're not coming," he said. "We'll have to call you Lonely Tenderfoot."

"They'll come!" I said. "They'll come!"

"You'll need to buy the right equipment," he said.

* * *

The Sacred Squirrel cost me a buck. It was carved from cedar. I blew into a hole in the tail. The air came out a hole in the back. Like a kazoo.

"Moo-oose," I said. "Dee-eer."

I crawled out, checking for deer and moose. My foot knocked a broomstick. My tepee toppled.

"Soup's on!" Mom yelled.

I snapped up the blanket and wrapped it around my shoulders and hiked into the house.

"You've got feathers in your hair," Dad said.

"I'm a brave." I emptied pockets—arrowhead, fish hooks, porcupine quills. Gobs of choke cherries.

"I could have stewed those," Mom said, tabling the turkey.

THE SHOWMAN

I collared Pete Johnson at tryouts. Gave him gifts: cape and gloves and top hat. "I bought myself this jacket," I said. It was red silk. "I thought I could be your assistant. You could levitate me or saw me in half or something."

Pete brought me onstage. I bowed.

"For my next trick," he said, "I will intercept his psychic waves." He blindfolded me. "He's thinking—" His voice went squeaky. "I sure wish I was Peter's sweetheart."

They hooted and clapped. Baton-twirling cheerleaders. Flag-twirling Scouts. Drama-clubbers costumed like characters from Oz.

"Enough!" the vice principal said.

* * *

From a taxidermist I bought eyes. Brown pupils, top-grade glass. Made for bucks.

Cosmetics I got from an undertaker. Flesh-tint for the face, rouge for lips and cheeks. For an extra dollar he yanked teeth from dentures. I glued them to the doll-dummy's gums.

The carpenter had crafted his head from pine, his body from tin. I dubbed him "Pete the Magician." When I pulled a pull-cord his mouth sprang open.

> ME: So, what can you do?
> PETE THE MAGICIAN: I can make you disappear.
> ME: The only thing you disappear is applause.
> PETE THE MAGICIAN: You know, you are next to an idiot.
> ME: You do look like one, don't you?

"No offense, kid," the carpenter said. "But you're not actually throwing your voice."

"Not yet," I said. "It takes six pages."

***

"A, E, I, O, U," I said. Jaws locked, teeth parted a hair. Standing before my bedroom mirror I read Edgar Bergen's book. I nailed most consonants. On "b" and "p" my lips moved. I said "vhee" and "fee" instead.

The book said: *To form words, make a sound like a bee's drone.*

I tensed my vocal cords. My cords cramped.

***

I ripped open boxes, dumped Cracker Jacks on my floor. Medals, wood puzzles, paper dolls—I tossed twenty prizes before I got it.

Boys! Boys! Boys!
Throw Your Voice!
Into a trunk, under the bed, under a table, back of the door, into a desk at school, or anywhere. You get lots of fun fooling the teacher, policemen, peddlers, and surprise and fool all your friends besides. THE

Grab Bag

VENTRILO or DOUBLE THROAT is a little instrument that fits in the mouth out of sight. Cannot be detected. It is used in connection with the above, and with the aid of this wonderful DOUBLE THROAT or VENTRILO you can become a ventriloquist imitating many kinds of birds, animals, etc.

It was yellow cellophane sandwiched in a leather half-moon. I popped it in my mouth. When I blew it made a high-pitch whistle. Blowing and tonguing I made bird trills. I tried talking. Ventrilo slid down my throat.

***

Mom's diagnosis: It'll come out. "Don't use it when it does," she said.

"It's your fault!"

She sshed me. She fiddled with my doll-dummy. Stripping my top sheet she hung it from the ceiling. She stood behind it. Shone a lamp.

"Do you think he should stop crying?" she said to the doll-dummy.

"Immediately," the doll-dummy said.
Shadowgraphs!

*　*　*

The janitor threw spotlights. They hit me from the front.

"No!" I said. "From the back! I need it from the back!"

The janitor wheeled out a Reflectoscope overhead projector. Hundred-watt bulb. He lowered the movie screen. It was black on the back.

"It won't work!" I said.

"A last-minute addition to our program," the vice principal said over the PA. Curtains waltzed open. Applause, then ahems.

"Just a minute." I rolled the Reflectoscope downstage, aimed it at the screen, stood in the beam.

> ME: Allow me to introduce my puppet.
> PETE THE MAGICIAN: I am not a fuffet! My name is Feter! I am the star of this fageant!

Our shadows blobs on the screen. Kids sniggering stage left.

"Wait!" I dropped the doll-dummy, stuck my hands in the light. Locking thumbs I flapped fingers. "This is a butterfly." I twined pointers. "This is a deer." And: "This is a turtle."

"Great one!" Some Boy Scout screamed: "How! How!"

"Use your imagination!" I screamed back.

THE JEWELER

Jason skimmed dead minnows and leeches and dumped them in the stinkbait pail.

I sat at the till. A man bought do-ball hooks. A man bought hoochy trolls.

A girl came in. Her hair was wavy and blond.

* * *

After supper Jason and I drove to Sophie's Lake. We hauled in Dad's minnow traps.

"She's beautiful," I said. "She looks like Carole Lombard."

"Her name's Sara," he said. He baited traps with dinner rolls, tossed them back. The sun dipping across the lake. Jack pines like fish bones.

* * *

I pulled my sheet over my head, put my flashlight on my pillow. The troll was a silver chain with five blades. For landing bass. I glued a green rhinestone to each blade. Then I laid it in my tackle box and pushed my tackle box under my bed.

* * *

Jason pulled the branches off the boat, hauled it from the woods. I paddled out.

"Are her ears pierced?" I said.

He shrugged, rigged his line with sinkers and a rubber crawler that smelled like pork.

Something struck. Took half his line. Zigzagged beneath us.

"It's a keeper!" he said. He played it out. I netted. It was a pike. It flipped out, flopped all over the boat. Oozing slime.

"Ugly bastard," he said. He dropped down and pinned it between his knees. He gouged out the eyes with a jackknife. He threw it back. Speared his hook through the eyes.

* * *

I pulled the weedguard off a Spinning Frog and glued a safety pin to the belly. I dipped Crippled Minnows in glue and dredged them in yellow glitter. Filed down hooks.

My flashlight died. In pitch black I rummaged through my tackle box.

Jason woke. He called from his room.

"Nothing," I said.

* * *

Jason dug a reel out of the junk box. He oiled the axle and the pawl. "Sara's coming so don't ask her any dumb questions."

She rode in front with him. I got the back of the truck. Bouncing down the ministry road, weeds fanning the engine.

She helped with traps. One had a little pike in it. Jason slit it and six minnows slopped out.

She oohed and shivered. Jason laughed and went for the boat.

I pulled a box from my jeans and gave it to her. *LIMP SPINNING LINE*, it said.

She opened it. "That's sweet," she said. "My first lures."

"They're not lures," I said. "That's a brooch. And that's a charm bracelet. And those are earrings. I made them myself."

Jason yelled. I went down to the shore.

"Think you could guard the truck awhile?" he said.

I shoved them off. I put on my sweater. I shone my flashlight at the lake. Walleye eyes glowed white. Then disappeared.

THE SINGING BRAKEMAN

The intern brought me pajamas and a cheesecloth handkerchief. A Dixie cup. I hawked into it. Nothing came up. Saliva.

> *As a teen Jimmie Rodgers repaired tracks in a railroad gang. Later he worked as a brakeman on the New Orleans and Northeastern line.*

I sat on the veranda and breathed the zero draught. An oldtimer in the next chair, ninety pounds, chest scarred from scalenotomies, thoracoplasties, pneumothoraxes, phrenic nerve crushes.
From doctors jimmying apart his ribs and spiling slime from his lungs.

> *After contracting TB Jimmie quit railroading. He toured Dixie as a minstrel in a medicine show.*

The doctor bronchoscoped me. He bombarded me with infrared and ultraviolet rays. Cooked my tubercle bacilli.

"It depends on your immune system," he said. "How you take care of yourself."

He injected me with two solutions. Sanocrysin, a gold preparation. Camphor, the stuff mothballs are made of.

"Everyone comes in contact with the bacteria," he said. "They're spores. They travel in the air."

"So I could have Jimmie Rodgers's spores?" I said.

Jimmie's first gold record was "Blue Yodel."
Most folks know it as "T for Texas."

After three weeks my lungs hadn't caseated or calcified. No sign of sputum. The ultraviolet treatments tanned me.

The sanatorium discharged me. Dad drove me home.

"You look like you've been south," he said.

Savile Row suits, boaters, spats, silk ties,

gold watches, diamond rings—Jimmie dressed to a tee. Unless he wore his railroad uniform, denim overalls and a brakeman's cap.

Mom took me downtown. At the Salvation Army I picked out denim overalls grimed with oil. A blue pinstripe suit, lining ripped, cuffs frayed.
"What about moths?" Mom said.
"Moths won't come near me," I said.

Against doctors' orders Jimmie continued to sing, smoke and drink alcohol. He travelled by train to a recording session in New York City.

We took the clothes to City Cleaners. In the window: *CLINIC FOR CLOTHES—WE STERILIZE!*
"How?" I asked the clerk. "How do you do it?"
The clerk toured me through the back room. Coffin-shaped presses. Torso-shaped molds. Tanks of chemicals—amyl acetate, benzine, chloroform, camphor.

Victor Recording Studio, New York City. Jimmie rises from his cot, musters air, wheezes into the mike. A needle etches his voice onto acetate discs. His last masters. "Whipping That Old TB" and "TB Blues."

My clothes came back in paper body bags. I put on my suit and a straw boater and strolled downtown. I had a coffee at the train station. I bought Black Cats, smoked under the water tower.

I coughed. Yellowish slime on my sleeve.

After his recording session Jimmie visited Coney Island. Freak shows, wax museums. He rode a roller coaster. On the tracks he had a fit of spasms, slipped into a coma. Days later he died.

I ran home, cigarettes squirrelled in my jacket lining.

My family doctor visited. He stethoscoped my chest. He whispered to Mom and Dad in the hall.

Midnight. Mississippi. Jimmie lay in a baggage car draped with black crepe. The conductor blew the whistle for ten minutes as the train rolled into the Meridian station.

Before dawn I dressed in my overalls. In a pillowcase I packed my shaving kit, my coin collection, my suit.

I snuck out. The sky like an X-ray of the moon. I bought a ticket on the 10 o'clock train to Toronto. From Toronto I'd hobo to Buffalo. Then New York City.

When City Cleaners opened I dropped off my suit. I waited at a diner across the street. Window seat, coffee.

Smoke clouded the cleaner's.

My matches.

Cigarettes, matches, a dryer, benzine—

The cleaner's roof blew. Walls caved, flames shot sky-high. I ran outside. I saw a tumbler drum spin like a Ferris wheel. Extractor bin carousels. Coat racks twisted like roller coaster track.

THE SUPER-HERO

Gangway for Captain Marvel!

At the arcade I bought a *Whiz* comic. I played Rifle Range! Shot fifteen coons.

I grabbed the knobs on Electric Energizer! Got zapped by fifty volts.

Mystic Pen Tells All! A fountain pen hung from wires. It jerked across a sheet of paper. The sheet slid down the chute:

"*Destiny Awaits.*"

Thunder. Sky flashing like a pinball backglass. I ran for home. Halfway there it started coming down.

* * *

Billy Batson peddling papers. Some man coaxes him onto a subway car. The subway zips

Billy to a cavern. There's a man on a throne. White hair, white beard.

"I know everything," the old man says. "I am Shazam!"

Lightning hits Billy. When the smoke clears he's twenty-five. He's got gold tights on.

Mom came in my room. She grabbed the comic and palmed my forehead.

I gulped aspirin.

* * *

My temp spiked. Scarlet streaked up my chest.

Dad drove me to Emergency. The doctor hooked me to a drip.

Days sleeping and sweating. The fever spread, pharynx to heart. The doctor taped electrodes to my chest.

"The ECG will trace your heartbeats," he said.

He turned it on. The pencil drew lightning bolts, then U-shapes.

The doctor wheeled a machine up to my bed. He put a steel cylinder in each of my hands.

A hundred amps of galvanic electricity.

* * *

Dr. Sivana's got a machine to silence radio signals. He wants fifty million dollars or he'll end broadcasts forever.

"Shazam!" Billy says. He flies to Sivana's lab. He hurls henchmen at machines. Coils, springs, control panels.

The doctor sat down on my bed. "Your heart's been scarred. Excitement could weaken it. Or worse."

He confiscated the comic. Ten minutes later an intern wheeled in the library cart. Plopped *Little Women* on my tray.

I shambled to the elevator. In the gift shop I bought a pad of paper, a pack of colored pencils.

* * *

The judge eyed some kid's crayon portrait of Batman. The Flash in pencil. Then the panels from my comic:

Scarlet fever's wasting Derek McCormack's heart. The doctor hooks him to an electrocardiograph.

Hospital lights die, then surge back on. Ten-thousand volts rip through Derek.

He rises from the smoke. All muscle. A red S *on his chest.*

"First prize goes to *Scarlatina the Immortal!*" He awarded me a silver dollar.

I walked out of the Craft Hall and up the midway. The Peterborough Ex. Cotton candy blue as electricity. Guys were firing rifles a t ducks and canvas clowns. Test Your Strength striker like a twenty-foot thermometer.

A man barking in a GRAPHOLOGY booth. "Have your handwriting analyzed!" he said.

I gave him the sheet from the arcade. *Destiny Awaits.*

"Who wrote it?" I said. "What does he want?"

THE NEWSHAWK

For the Ex, one guy got the Grandstand and Devil Drivers, another got the Manufacturer's Building.

I got Livestock.

"Best Livestock reporter ever," I told the editor.

***

"We can't keep up with the boom," the horse director said.

I scratched it shorthand. Every stall in the horse barn was occupied. Race horses shared the sheep barn. Heavy horses shoehorned into a Bingo tent.

"They laughed at me when I said we'd need a new barn this year," he said.

"Are you saying," I said, "that you suspect a misappropriation of funds?"

"No," he said.

* * *

A hundred Holsteins. Gassing.

"Best section in the history of the fair," the cow director said. "The Colonel was going to bring his Hereford herd. Then his wife had an accident. She's laid up in Nicholl's Hospital."

"A victim," I said, "of an over-zealous competitor eager to knock the Colonel out of the running?"

"No," he said.

* * *

Swine scuttled across the show ring. *Sold!*—to Dominion, A&P, Foodway.

"Swine fall into two classes," the swine director said. "Bacon Breeds and Special Commercial."

"And yet Canada Packers supplies the trophy," I said. "Do I smell conflict of interest?"

"No," he said.

* * *

A White Rock pullet won best female. A Bantam cock best male.

"And we've got an exceptional exhibit of pigeons," the poultry director said.

"Whoopee." I wandered aisles, copying names. Aylesbury ducks. Cochin China fowls. Silver spangled Polish.

"You a detective?" a fellow said.

"Examiner," I said, flashing my press card.

He said, "I got a story."

* * *

I ran it by the editor.

"This old guy raises a turkey," the editor said. "Then days before the fair, it flies off?"

"Stolen!" I said. "What I want to know is: Why? What was so special about that turkey? Who didn't want him to win?" I said: "It's got poultry ring written all over it!"

He tossed me out. I kicked dirt up the midway. Pirate flags stretched on prize racks. Carnies offering up guns, darts, hardballs.

"Winner every time," they said.

THE FREAK

The manual said: *Guaranteed to cure.*

It looked like a slide projector. I unpacked it and plugged it in. The Spectro-Ray 2000.

I undid my shirt. Beams of light between my nipples. My skin went red, then blue, then yellow.

This, the manual said, warmed alveoli, liquefying tuberculosis bacteria.

A rap at the door. My manager. "You got a customer," he said.

"I'm taking the cure." I spun the knob to *HIGH*. The beam broke into a million white dots. Light cells, the manual said. To replace cells ravaged by the disease.

"He ain't going away," my manager said.

I stomped out of the trailer, through the tent. The entrance was roped off. A sign chained to the bally said *NEXT SHOW AT.*

My customer was a little kid, a real rube, straw hat and galluses. "You the Living X-Ray?" he said.

I sucked in air. Skin shrink-wrapped my ribs. My heart beat against it, my liver fluttered. The lump in my bowels was lunch. A slice of toast. I was down to ninety pounds.

I took a fit. Coughed up my weight in sputum. It was lawn-colored. Bloody swirls. "Show's over," I said, wiping my lips.

"I don't feel any better," he said.

"You're not supposed to. I'm the one getting paid."

He rolled back his sleeves. Up his arms an angry red rash. Skin scaling.

"If you want a job you'll have to see the manager," I said. "But frankly you'll need better than that. The Human Alligator's got scales all over. Even the Man-Woman's got a worse complexion."

"Mom sent me to town," he said, "to get the X-ray treatment to burn off the ringworm but then I seen the rides and then I guess I blew most of the money but then I seen the sign for the Living X-Ray and I thought maybe you could—" He got teary. His lip curled. "Forget it," he said.

Candy floss in spinning bins. Weenies roasting on weenie Ferris wheels. I walked him down the foodway to a french fry stand. I doused vinegar on his arms. I poured it down his bib, soaked his shirt, socks, scalp.

"Old wives' cure," I said.

He wailed. The ringworm flared. Fairgoers crowded around, scarfing popcorn and peanuts.

"What are you gawking at?" I said. I dropped my pants. They dropped their food. Paper cones like party hats trampled into the grass.

THE CARNY

"It's shit work," I said. "Shit pay."

"I'd do it for nothing," he said. "I just can't go home or—"

"Let me guess. Your pa will kill you?"

He spat. Light showing through the holes in his jeans. "More like I'll kill him."

I walked him up the hanky-pank. "The midway's the hanky-pank," I said.

* * *

He spun the Wheel-of-Fortune.

"Some guys'll call it the Plush Wheel," I said. "Or Flat Wheel."

Under the counter I pressed a pedal tied to a string. The string dragged the axle and the wheel slowed up with the flapper pointing to *TRY AGAIN*.

"G," I said. "Gaff. Fix. Rig."

* * *

"First off," I said, "call them stores. This here's a Block Store, also known as a Tilyou."

Three iron milk cans on a platform. He winged a baseball, missed by a mile.

"The balls are weighted," I said. "There's magnets in the platform."

The next store had a row of baskets tilted upward. He pitched a ball underhanded. It trampolined out.

"Five-ounce balls," I said. "The bottom of a peach basket's tighter than a virgin's ass."

He pitched again.

"Dime a pitch. Pitch till you win."

* * *

"You got your Count-and-Peek Store—"

Steel fish rusting in a trough. He dropped in a line baited with a magnet.

"There's a hundred fish in there. Two are marked #2."

Grab Bag

He lands #1.

"That's flash," I said, pointing to the prizes. Plaster statues. They were pyramided, big ones on the top row. "You lure them in with that. Then give them slum."

Bottom row: Statuettes. Bamboo canes. Tin whistles.

* * *

I watched from the crowd. He called for bets. The table was round and marked up with numbers, like a clock. There was a hole at every hour. A lady put money on the ten hole. Two oldtimers played the four and eight.

In the middle sat a glass bowl. A mouse hopping like a gas-pump canary underneath.

"Wait!" Some kid in a straw hat pushed to the front, laid a coin at 6 o'clock.

He gaffed it like I told him: Reach under the counter, then touch 3 o'clock. Leave a little drop. Mice love vinegar.

He lifted the bowl. The mouse shot for 6 o'clock.

Straw hat took a toaster.

I pulled him off the wheel. "You gaff it?"

"It was the rube!" he said. "He reeked of vinegar!"

I walked him Spanish down the alley behind the stores. Couple of operators met me back of the freak-show tents. They knocked him down.

"That your scam?" I said. "Throw the game and split the take with your pal?"

Out of his pockets I pulled a card that said *Peterborough Examiner*.

He starts whimpering: "Let me go and I swear I won't write a word."

"Here's the rules." I kicked him. "Ribs—three points." I stomped his hand. "Fingers—two points." He screamed bloody murder. I kicked his head. "Nothing for teeth. Too easy."

THE SCULPTOR

I made a pig. Airbrushed it blue. Glued green glitter eyes. I scratched my initials and the words: *Prize by.*

I made all the carnival's flash. Plaster statues cast in metal molds. There were red cats. Yellow elephants. Budgies the size of owls.

A carny stuck his head in my tent. "Forget it, kid," he said. "We can't give the stuff away."

* * *

Fish rusting in the Fish Pond. Carnies smoking, leaning on laydowns, spinning their wheels.

Not a mark playing games. I walked back. There were a few on the foodway. A few riding rides.

It was mark city at the sideshow. Banners breaking in the breeze. *See The Wolf Boy! Live—The Living*

X-Ray! Beware! Spidora, Half-Woman, Half-Spider!

I slipped in the side. The freaks were hawking souvenirs. Autographed photos. Life stories printed on postcards.

"I've got one on my pinky!" said Stanley, World's Tallest Giant. He held up rings. They were die cast, big as bracelets. "Biggest in the world!" he said. "Two bucks apiece!"

Marks stood on tiptoe to hand him dough.

* * *

The freaks were sleeping. I crept through the tent to the blow-off. The blow-off's where they kept punks. Punks are pickled babies.

I stole some. Dumped them out in my tent. One brainless, one with two heads, one with spina bifida. I held them over a hot plate. They softened up. They were wax. Fakes.

I made molds. Poured in plaster. When it hardened I slapped on paint.

I took speed.

* * *

"Stanley the Giant's!" A carny held up a plaster shoe I'd made. Size 19. "Win the biggest shoe in the world!"

Marks crowded around. They pitched balls at the Cat Rack. Yanked strings at the String Store.

"Big winner!" a carny called. He gave out a plaster hand. "Genuine duplication of Stanley the Giant's hand! Biggest in the world!"

Marks lined up at the Hoop Toss and the Knife Rack and the Country Store. Marks shooting corks at metal ducks.

"Got more of that flash?" a carny said.

It smelled like footlongs. I weaved through the crowd, ducked into my tent. The molds were in pieces, stretched, wrung, hacked.

A kewpie caught me square in the face. It shattered. My teeth like hopscotch markers on the ground.

I fell. Stanley fell on top of me. Yanked down my pants. Plowed his dick in.

After a while he grunted. Buckled up. "Biggest in the world," he said.

I touched my hole. Spongy flesh stuck out. Semen like plaster running down my thigh.

THE NURSE

I chalked a grid on his scalp, then rubber-cemented electrodes to his central and occipital zones.

"Be hard to sleep with a pretty thing like you in here," he said.

"I won't be." I shut the door behind me. The electrode wires ran along the floor, into the electroencephalograph machine. I switched it on. The drum rolled. Pencils drew brain waves on paper. O1 and O2 caught alpha rhythms, twelve cycles per second.

"You sure you don't want to crawl in with me?" he yelled.

"Go to sleep!"

* * *

C3 and C4 etched wobbly lines, odd bursts, negative spikes. Dreams.

I made a note in the report. At midnight I drifted down the Cardiac wing. The lobby dark, gift shop locked-up. Santa tea cozies and silk poinsettias jollied the display case. Nurse dolls with snap-shut eyes.

Vending machines humming in the cafeteria. I bought a bag of peanuts. Insert dime, press C4.

* * *

Past 4 he slipped into Stage C sleep. Steep spikes slalomed the paper. He ripped off an electrode. I reglued it.

The PA: *"Staff to Emergency."*

The girls in Admitting had a punch bowl of eggnog on a gurney. We toasted the season—orderlies, X-ray technicians, the surgeon from Intensive Care. Santa string-'em-outs overhead. The eye chart a Christmas tree of letters.

* * *

I woke him at 6.

"Did I sleepwalk?" he said.

With rubbing alcohol I scrubbed the rubber cement from his scalp. He dressed, left. I caught the city bus. It was packed with night girls. Drowsing.

* * *

I drank warm milk. A shot of brandy. I taped my curtains to the windowpane, blindfolded myself and pulled covers over my head.

I was wide awake. Sally Ann Santas shaking bells on the street below.

I splashed my face with ice water. I tucked my Christmas list in my purse.

Dresses in the dress shop. Hats in the hat shop. A brass bed showcased in Turnbull's Department Store. Goosedown duvet. Feather pillows. Throws.

I went in. En route to Linens I passed Jewelry. Silver chains like brain waves. I held an alpha rhythm in twisted silver. I checked the mirror. Gasped.

"Is there a beauty shop?" I said.

THE HELP

I cleared the table, scraped plates, swept.

Mrs. Turnbull tinkled her bell.

It was mint velvet with fitted shoulders and beads on the bust. A furbelow.

"Lelong," she said, twirling for her mirror. "From Creeds in Toronto."

I nodded like I knew.

"Would you check my makeup?" she said.

I aimed the vanity lamp. I powdered the base of her neck, redrew her right eyebrow.

I carried the pot in from the porch. The cold had congealed the fat. I skimmed it off, drained broth, threw out bones and giblets.

I lit the stove. The matchbook said *DIPLOMA*.

* * *

In a week the booklet came. In a month the exam. How are short bobs singed? What kind of dye should never be used to color eyebrows and eyelashes? *T or F: Infection may be caused by improper use of tweezers.*

I wrote out my answers and a check to the school and posted them at the post office. I picked up pork chops, then headed for the Turnbull's. By running the flame of a wax taper over ends of hair. Aniline derivative dye. T.

Snowbanks glittering like eye shadow.

* * *

"It's for real," I said, showing my diploma.

Mrs. Turnbull perfumed her wrists. Sniffed.

"I was hoping, I mean do you think, could Mr. Turnbull try me in his store. Once?"

* * *

The Salon was on Second, off Women's Wear. I wore a white smock. I swept around chairs. Watered ferns.

A lady dinged the service bell. "Do I need an appointment?" she said.

Astringent shrunk the bags beneath her eyes. A bleach pack whitened plukes. "I'm not usually this bad," she said. "It's the night duty. I'm the only nurse in my wing."

I suggested ringlets. I trimmed and tapered her hair, blocked it into squares and triangles. Moving from scalp to end I flat-wrapped them around steel rods.

I excused myself. In the laundry room I checked my booklet: *Cover the rods with curlpapers, tinfoil and flannel.*

This I did. I doused her scalp with ammonium carbonate.

She coughed and cried.

"Bear with me," I said, sponging trickles from her brow.

I wheeled her beneath the permanent waving machine, a chandelier of wires. I clamped wires to the rods on her head. I fired up the electric generator. The voltmeter needle hiccupped, then died. I knelt and shook the machine. I upped the heat. 400 degrees   . 450 degrees

Smoke. I spun around. Clamps were sparking, wires glowing orange. The nurse had her head thrown back. Snoring.

THE SALESCLERK

"I chose Rosefield," the owner said.
"From Furniture?" I said.

* * *

Roger Rosefield, the new Display Director, trimmed the main window with bunny dolls.

I measured some man's feet.

Roger hung spun-glass clouds, a pink crepe backdrop. He arranged dyed eggs on a carpet of cellophane grass.

I fetched size 12 slippers. I fluoroscoped the man's foot. The leather looked smoky, his bones black.

* * *

The stench was like sulphur and old shoes. It crept from the main window to Cosmetics and beyond. Perfume girls atomized ounce upon ounce.

Roger tore out his display. I swung by the owner's office.

"I would never have used real eggs," I said.

* * *

I fluoroscoped some man's feet.

Roger carpeted the floor of the window in daisies.

Thousand-watt spotlights. They browned the daisies in under an hour.

I popped by the office. "Any idiot would've used crepe flowers," I said. "Or sealing wax."

* * *

Roger ensembled child mannequins dressed in domino masks. Twenty jack-o'-lanterns. A backdrop of cornstalks.

I pyramided shoe boxes. I spied a dime-size sore on my upper arm. It was purplish, tender to touch.

I shoved my arm in the fluoroscope. The spot vanished. My hand a crib scythe.

* * *

The sore blackened. I poulticed it with bread. It grew triangular. I rubbed it with zinc salve. It crusted and oozed and stuck to my shirt.

Halloween day I ran up to the hospital. A doctor fingered the sore. He inspected my scalp. He shone a flashlight in my eyes.

He X-rayed me. My spine a chalky zipper. Lumps ghosting my neck and ribcage.

"Tumors," he said. He said ultraviolet rays or coal tar or bruises could have caused them. Or bacteria: He said when cancerous tumors are ground into juice and injected into rabbits, the rabbits develop the same kind of tumor.

"Can't you stop it?" I said.

The purpling sky. I trudged back to the store, pocket full of painkillers. In the window janitors were waving butterfly nets at moths flickering in and out of cornstalks. The jack-o'-lanterns puckered, their insides specked with blueblack mold.

Derek McCormack

The owner met me in Accessories. "Rosefield's out," he said. "You're in."

* * *

I curtained the main window. I bought glow-in-the-dark paint and brushed it onto merchandise.

Next evening the owner and comptroller and department managers massed on the sidewalk. Pedestrians paused.

I drew back the curtains. It was a Night before Xmas scene—tinselled tree, toy train, dolls. Child mannequins in nightshirts and caps. All spotlit green and red.

Cars slowed. Pedestrians clapped.

A breaker switched. Lights died. The paint fluoresced. Suddenly the children were X-rays. Luminous limbs, skulls. Egg-shaped tumors glowing green between their ribs.

THE GHOST

There was a Christmas tree in the main window. A toy train shunting between gifts.

"Wow!" I said.

I walked downstreet, planted myself at the corner window. Stared at gowns—silks, velvets, taffetas—washed with red floods.

Two women stopped. Looked. Squinted.

I slipped away to a row of shadowboxes. In each box a beauty item. I stared at a compact, an eye shadow case, a snowman built of puffs.

Folks leaned over my shoulder to see what I was seeing.

I rounded the corner. Tall, narrow windows flanked the east entrance. End runs. Robot elves shovelled snow. I pressed my nose to the glass.

"Anything good?" asked a man.

In the main window the Santa Claus Express

was still chugging around its track. I pointed, tapped the glass. "Wow!" I said.

I stared at gowns in the corner.

I stared at shadowboxes.

I stared at end runs.

I did three more circuits. At noon I went inside. "I'm the window gazer," I said.

The Display Director told me to change. I combed my hair the other way. In Men's Wear I put on a different jacket and tie. And spectacles. The lenses were nothing. Clear glass.

Cosmetics girls ran by. They wore lab coats. Squealed.

I followed them to the change area. A crowd was building, shoppers and staff.

I slipped through the security door. Beyond the guard's office stretched a narrow hall lined with two-way mirrors. I tiptoed. The first change room was empty. In the second, an old man.

The third contained Bing Crosby. He centered his tie. Checked how he looked from the side, from the front, from behind. In his skivvies.

He put on pants, breathed deep and threw open the door.

Grab Bag

The crowd pressed in. Flashbulbs blew.

* * *

Next morning. 8 a.m. Staring at the toy train.

A store detective grabbed my shoulder. "Beat it," he said. "You're fired." Then: "Fairy."

He pulled out a photo. Bing grinning. A ghost floating behind. Me. My dick in my hand.

THE SUITOR

Eight inches. Cylindrical steel. A carrier dropped down. In it: a bill for pumps and ten dollars.

I stamped the bill, broke the ten, threw change in the carrier and shot it down the tube to Women's Shoes.

I was the cashier at Turnbull's Department Store. My office overlooked second- and third-floor galleries. I watched the lady pocket her change, the clerk bag the pumps.

I scanned down to the Main Level. Men's Department.

Kevin.

* * *

Wall-to-wall pneumatic tubes, each one two and

a quarter inches in diameter, seamless steel braced in creosoted wood ducts. Incomings and outgoings linked to every department in the store.

The system was simple. A carrier arrived from Furniture. One couch, on credit. I tubed back a receipt. I tubed another carrier. I was pretending to file statements when Kevin knocked, rose petals in his hands.

"Who sent these?" he said.

"I'd like to know," I said. "I just stepped out for a moment."

***

My carrier flew toward him at forty miles an hour. His receiving gate was closed. My carrier piled up an air cushion ahead of it. The cushion forced his gate. My carrier dropped into his scoop at a mile an hour.

Peering over my desk I watched him jog up.

"I don't know," I said. "I have things to do."

"Was it Susan in Accounting?" he said. "Or Glenda?"

Candy hearts.

* * *

Pneumatic pressure produced by air compressors and rotary blowers. Kevin was pinning struts into collars. I sent out my carrier.

The carrier jammed. Air screeched. Customers stopped shopping and clerks waved their arms.

I called down to the basement, had janitors double the pressure in the tubes. I had the pressure reversed and reversed back again.

I cut power. I jammed a pole down the tube.

The owner blew in. "Is it the customer in Men's Wear?" he said. "How much change do we owe him?"

"We don't," I said. "There is no customer. Sir."

"Was it a memo?" he said. "Where from?"

"I'll take care of it," I said. I jammed a plumber's snake down the tube.

"From you?" the owner said.

I hit the carrier. Heard it pop open. Spill.

I snatched my coat, bounded down escalators. Bolted past Kevin.

"What's going on?" he said. Then compressors kicked in. His gate flew open. Gold glitter sprayed out, settled as far off as China.

THE CONFECTIONER

His cock fattening. Semen like egg white.

* * *

"She'll love it," Mrs. Turnbull said. "She's sweet sixteen."

I'd covered a cherry poundcake with chains, scrolls, loops, garlands, piping, overpiping, diamond threading. To top it off—it was nearly July—daisies made with meringue.

Mr. Turnbull wrote a check.

* * *

With a no. 8 tube I spun nail roses. They were sugar, an inch tall, six petals apiece. I planted them on his ass. His ass looked like a bathing cap.

I ate the roses. Tongued his hole.

* * *

"Will it serve eight?" Mrs. Turnbull asked.

A Halloween cake frosted with cocoa and fondant, dotted with pulled-sugar pumpkins, cornstalks and witches' heads.

I rang it through the till.

Mr. Turnbull shook his head. "Parties coming out my ears."

* * *

With a camel-hair brush I glazed his nipples, his bellybutton. I buttered his cock.

* * *

I pulled cakes from the window display. "I've got a Santa Claus," I said. "And wreaths. Holly or poinsettia."

"What's the Christmas tree?" Mrs. Turnbull said.

"Fruitcake."

"As long as it's sweet," Mr. Turnbull said.

* * *

Streetlamps throwing cornets of light. Streets dead.

I locked up. Bowls stacked in the kitchen. Meringue drying flinty. XXXX sugar.

From the fridge I pulled a block of marzipan. The shape of his cock molded into it.

I licked the length. I dropped my drawers, fingered my asshole.

I screamed.

* * *

After lubricating me the doctor inserted a steel syringe. "I'm filling the rectum with air," he said.

He snapped off his gloves. *"Condylomata acuminata,"* he said. "Venereal warts. Very contagious. Very common among catamites."

He lathered his hands. "I will treat you to the best of my ability," he said. "Then I will never treat you again."

Ass throbbing I stormed up Charlotte Street. *J. TURNBULL'S* in neon.

I stormed through Cosmetics, up the escalators to 4. President's office. "Where's John?" I said.

The secretary rose. "Mr. Turnbull is away on business."

"What kind of business? Where?"

I farted. Jelly smeared my cheeks.

THE ELF

"Sloppy," the manager said. "Look at the smudges." He crumpled my sheet.

I dipped my pen. Wrote: *Things are jolly here at the North Pole.*

The guy at the next desk slipped me a rubber. "I'm Blake," he said.

* * *

"'Nautty?'" the manager said. "It's spelled n-a-u-g-h-t-y." He crumpled my sheet. "Are you s-t-u-p-i-d?"

Kids sent lists. *Dear Santa.* I had to send letters back: *I hope you've been a nice boy and not bad.*

"Don't let him get to you," Blake said, rolling over in his chair. "He thinks he's such a tough guy."

Grab Bag

* * *

A horse is sure a big wish. Are you sure you don't want a doggie?

"Do we sell doggies?" the manager said. He picked up the Christmas wish book. Threw it at me. "If you can't do the job," he said, "I'll find someone who can."

I started over. *A horse sure is a big wish. Wouldn't you rather have a Steiff horse doll, item 8044, $4.95? Or a cast-iron horse and buggy, item 9652, $8.95?*

"It took me time to catch on," Blake said. "There are tricks."

* * *

A Visit from St. Nicholas. A Christmas Carol. The Selfish Giant. Blake gave me books. "Go through those," he said. "If you find yourself in a jam, lift a line or two."

'Twas the night before Christmas, I wrote. *And what to your wondering eyes will appear? A mahogany chessboard with bakelite queens.*

The manager picked it up. Handed it back.

"Whaddya want?" he said. "A pat on the head?"

Blake winked.

* * *

Chutes shut. Dust covers on addressographs. The manager swept through the mailroom, killing lights. "Wrap it up," he said, exiting.

Blake blotted a letter. Spritzed it with peppermint perfume. He dropped it in the Out bag. The bag was brimming. "Done?" he said.

My hand a charley horse.

He grabbed it. He pulled back my fingers. They cracked. "My first Christmas," he said, "I thought my arm would fall off."

He kneaded my palm. His thumbs rubbed my lines. "Truth is," he said, "I'm glad you started working here. It was kind of lonely. Not talking to anyone all day."

His hands slick with sweat. "It's worse around Christmas," he said. "Being on your own. You know?"

"I've got something for you," I said.

***

"Ink blots," the psychiatrist said. He dropped cards on the desk. "Ten in total. I made them by squirting ink on a piece of paper and folding it in half. You probably played this game when you were a tot—it's called Blotto."

"Am I in trouble?" Blake said.

"When I give you a card," the psychiatrist said, "please hold it in both hands like this. Tell me what you see there, what it means to you. There are no right or wrong answers."

Blake picked up a card. "Can I pick it up?"

"As you wish," the psychiatrist said.

"I don't know," Blake said, a husk in his throat. "Nothing. A mask. Is that right?"

"Whatever you say," the psychiatrist said.

"I can't tell," Blake said. He picked up the next card. "Two men, maybe. Or a fountain."

A ballerina. Smoke. A judge's wig. A beautiful gown. A Christmas tree with globes.

The psychiatrist glanced sidelong at the mirror.

"Jesus," the manager said. He was standing behind the two-way. "How'd you know?"

I shrugged. "He tried to make me go fairy, too."

He clamped my shoulder. "You did good, kid."

I thanked him. I could smell his talc. His aftershave. He was beautiful. Blue eyes. Blue shaven. Lips pink as nipples.

He said: "I'm sending you to Happyland."

* * *

I blew up a pencil balloon. With my finger I poked in the knot. I made a twist for the head. Double end-tied the nipple. The nipple was a nose.

"What is it?" said a little girl.

I called it a reindeer. I made penguins, rabbits, bees. Poodles floating over their leashes.

THE PARTY-POOPER

Carl asked me to his party. Mom took me shopping after school. Turnbull's had a wizard costume with silver moons and stars.

"Girl stuff," I said.

We walked to Eaton's. Some sad-sack was panhandling by the penny arcade.

"Help the blind?" he said.

I stuck out my tongue. I stretched my mouth out wide with my fingers.

"Beat it, kid," he said.

* * *

Next time I saw him he was acting deaf and dumb. Lips zipped, hands flapping.

I let go a couple raspberries.

"Git!" he said.

* * *

He was on crutches. A can at his feet.
I grabbed the can and ran.

* * *

I went as him to the party. A can tied around my neck. Joey Parker won the prize for best costume. He had on a tinfoil crown. Called himself "Prince of Halloween."

"That's stupid," I said. "There's no such thing. You're retarded."

Carl's mom sent me home. Mom and Dad sent me to bed. When they fell asleep I climbed out my window. I egged Carl's porch and ran. I egged Joey Parker's porch. I egged downtown, soaped the window at Turnbull's. Wrote, *I AM THE PRINCE!*

THE CURATOR

"The grand tour," I said. "On the house."

He'd come in chanting: *"Help the blind?"* Now he looked at me. Looked around. "Where's the sweet shop?"

"The sweet shop's history." I jerked my thumb at the show window. I'd written the name in soap. *Crime Hall of Fame.* "Too bad you can't see."

He grinned. Teeth brown and yellow like Indian corn.

I slapped his back, guided him to the candy counter. In it lay a cape. "This little beauty belonged to none other than Jack the Ripper. I bought it off a bobby in London, England."

"No shit," he said.

I pointed to a jellybean jar. A hand pickled in alcohol. "Jesse James. His uncle was a barber in Tombstone, Arizona. He preserved it in barbicide.

You will notice the trigger finger is still cocked to shoot."

Down the aisle sat a hat on a barrel.

"John Dillinger's. See the gun flash on the brim? G-man put that there." On the next barrel lay a pair of hose. No runs but lots of dried blood. "Bonnie Parker's. They're pure silk. Clyde bought those in Kansas City."

I showed him Ma Barker's pet cat. The snake that bit Cleopatra. Both stuffed. "Got those from the Smithsonian in Washington. Swapped them for Lizzie Borden's axe."

At the back I had brains floating in Mason jars. "Leopold and Loeb. Try if you will to imagine the sheer evil they contain."

I passed him one. The fool fumbled it. Smash. Brain skidding across the floor. He grabbed at it, tearing brain folds. A glass shard sliced his thumb.

"Do you realize what you've destroyed?" I said. "The loss to history? To science?"

* * *

That night I bought another brain at the abattoir.

***

Something. I opened an eye and checked the clock. 1 a.m. The radio spitting fuzz. I shut it off, swilled the toddy I'd poured during *The Shadow*. Started to slip off when the sound came again: *rap-rap-rap*.

I got up, stumbled through the museum.

The beggar.

"Two hundred," he said. "Two hundred bucks and you can have my jacket." He shed it. Shivering. The wind was minus-something. "How's about a hundred? Then we're even for the brain."

"You been drinking?"

"I just killed a kid."

"Yeah? Did you kidnap the Lindbergh baby too?"

"I seen him soaping the department store and I just meant to choke him a little." He wobbled. "He went blue."

"Just one kid? Hundred bucks is a little steep. Why don't you come back when you've got a few under your belt."

I slammed the door and scuffled back to bed.

* * *

Then the daily paper. Radio news flash. I called the cops. They staked out the work room, the upstairs flat.

I sat inside the door. At twilight shopkeepers winched awnings. The fellow at the fur shop hauled his grizzly in for the night.

A plainclothes-man stopped by. "You're staying open."

The sun went. Kids flooded the street. Vampires, cowboys, ghosts. Pillowcases full of sweets.

Jack-o'-lanterns exit signs.

THE MAGICIAN

The attendant tanked me up. "Buck-fifty," he said.

I swallowed a length of string. Five razor blades. When I drew the blades from my mouth they were strung together.

"Buck-fifty," the attendant said.

* * *

I linked solid steel rings. I showed my palm, made a fist, then produced sixteen silks.

This at a Home for the Aged. The Aged applauded.

"Coppers, nickels, what have you!" I said, passing around my top hat. I made a newspaper cone and poured their coins in.

Abracadabra!—silk flowers sprang out.

I bowed, backed away.

"Where's my money?" Some old bat.

* * *

The girl with polio, the boy TB.

I conjured hypodermics from a sickness bag. I cut a tensor bandage and rejoined the halves.

In the hall I said, "I haven't eaten much today."

The nurse scared up a sandwich. I wolfed it down in the Intensive Care waiting room. Jesus in oils. A litho of King George. A poster offering a reward. Thousand dollars cash. It said: *WHO KILLED LITTLE TIM?*

"Terrible," the nurse whispered.

* * *

"What is the meaning of this?" the father said. "Who are you?"

I swept past him, through the front room, the kitchen. A ship's compass hung on the den wall. I waved my arms and the compass needle quavered, *N* to *E*.

"Tim says he's fine," I said. "He says he misses you. He says he's watching over you."

The mother started bawling. "Send him our love," she said.

The father insisted, so I buckled. Took ten dollars.

In the car I unhooked magnets from my sleeves.

* * *

The newspaper said: *Dear Mother, at home in Peterborough, peacefully, in her ninetieth year . . .*

A black crepe scarf had been knotted to the door knocker.

"You don't know me," I said, "but I have a message for you. From the beyond."

The daughter led me to the parlor. She dimmed kerosene lamps and lit candles. I ripped up her mother's obituary. When I opened my hands it was restored. I laid a blank slate on a table. I waved a silk.

"Of course," I said, "donations allow me to continue my work."

* * *

Flashpaper flashed. Smoke pellets smoked. "Begone, ghost!" I bellowed.

The farmer hollered from his stoop. "What if it comes back?"

"Full refund!"

High beams blazing I sped down a dirt road, sheered onto another, another. Farmhouse. Frame church. Tombstones like cash register flags.

Thud. The car bucked over cabbages. Fifty-odd heads dotted the road.

The motor conked out. The gas gauge hit *E*.

"Shit." I crammed the money in my sock, buttoned my tuxedo and set off, cape rustling like leaves. Past Halloween high jinks: A scarecrow swinging from an elm. A bed frame bridging a ditch. An outhouse smack dab in the road.

A man. He came staggering toward me, a sack slung over his shoulder. Two feet sticking out the top.

"Hey, Mandrake," he said. "Meet Schmoo."

THE EMCEE

I told them that in Buffalo, New York, Halloween had for years been characterized by broken streetlights, false fire alarms, overturned automobiles, sawed-down telephone poles, streets barricaded with debris and flooded by open fire hydrants.

"In 1933," I said, "I was hired by the Buffalo Halloween Committee." The Committee, I told them, had comprised representatives from the YMCA, YWCA, Boy Scouts, Girl Scouts, Camp Fire Girls, Hi-Y and Tri-Hi-Y, Volunteers of America, Parent-Teacher Associations, Church Federation, Veterans of Foreign Wars and Auxiliary, Civic and Commerce Association, Ladies of the Cemetery Association, Elks, Kiwanis, Masons, various department stores, Dennison and Beistle and other manufacturers of quality holiday novelties.

"Our common desire," I said, "was to create a new, constructive Halloween tradition for children.

"And we achieved it."

I told them of ghoul parades, cemetery picnics, funeral processions bearing caskets full of sweets. Father-son parties featuring horror movies and boxing and ghost shows by professional magicians. Mystery hikes and treasure hunts in the woods, outdoor wiener roasts, cornhusking bees.

"But there are many other options," I said. I listed some: a Druid's Festival featuring a bonfire and a half circle of stones open to the sun; a Hobo Party involving an abandoned lot and a freight car and boys fashioning tin-can noisemakers and frying-pan rattlers; a Gypsy Campfire complete with a fortune-teller and an accordionist playing "My Little Gypsy Sweetheart" and "The Raggle-Taggle Gypsies O"; or a Kidnap Party. Girls are locked up in an old barn or garage and boys have to rescue them by tracing a trail of clues.

"The result," I said, "a twenty-percent drop in boy trouble. A renewed spirit of community. And I needn't tell you that had a plan such as mine been in place last Halloween, certain tragic incidents might well have been avoided."

City Council blessed my plan.

* * *

A two hundred count ghost in the linen shop window. Cheddar pumpkins in the cheese shop display.

At Eaton's window trimmers were hanging a backdrop of black crepe.

I rapped on the plate glass. "Crepe is velvety on one side!" I yelled. "The velvety side faces out! Always!"

I crossed the street.

* * *

"We'll post a sign," I said. *"BEWARE OPEN GRAVE!"*

City workers jackhammered asphalt. Trenchers dug. The foreman made a cordon of pylons. They were shaped like witches' hats.

"Nice touch," I said.

I pasted cut-outs to car headlights, streetlamp globes, Esso pumps. Black triangle eyes. Black circle noses. Black cog teeth.

When the orange gas bubbled up—
Gas pumpkins.

* * *

I stepped into it. Twirled around. The dress was slit up the back and corded. Orange crepe printed with black cats on broomsticks. "I recommend basting and an X-stitch hem," I said.

A Domestic Science class at the high school. All ears.

"It's simple, versatile, effective," I said. "For wizards, use a star pattern. For a skeleton, go all black and add fabric tape ribs."

I handed out patterns. S, M, L, XL. Later, addressing the Shop Class, I distributed patterns for lawn cut-outs. Plywood scarecrows and black cats and goblins.

"Plant them in gardens along your Scenic Route," I said. "Crossing guard signs make nice pumpkins."

They set to jigsawing. Sawdust pale as cornstalks.

***

My fingers grazed old furs and raw liver nailed to the walls. "More liver," I said. Further along the corridor I heard thunder. A cowbell clanging under a running faucet. "Increase the pressure," I said. I kicked chains, bed springs, tin pans, cornstalks, and lengths of hose strewn on the floor. Damp hairnets cobwebbed my face.

"I want a man at every stairway, doorway, and stunt," I said. Employees culled from each department stood before me in the furnace room at Turnbull's Department Store. "Working in utter darkness," I said, "with hundreds of boys screaming and yelling, only older men with a lot of common sense are adequate to handle a Haunted House."

I marched volunteers to the boiler room. A white scrim hung from the ceiling. We watched two shadowgraphs—doctor and deceased. With scissors and tongs the doctor removed an intestine, passed it to me.

"Just sausage," I said.

***

I snipped the ribbon with scissors. "I am proud to declare the Museum of Fun officially open!"

I mingled with the boys, county Cubs and Scouts. They'd constructed ten booths. The first had a sign: *Performing Dogs!*

I drew back the curtain. Links of wienerwurst swayed on strings.

The idea came straight from the "Dime Museum Fun" chapter of my instructional book, *Halloween Carnival Time!*, which the local bookstore had stocked in numbers. Other ideas the troops employed:

> – *The Boy Who Reads Under Water* (a boy reading while a bucket hangs over his head)
> – *The World Famous Twenty-Four Carat Ring* (a circle of carrots)
> – *The Swimming Match* (matches floating in a fishbowl)
> – *The One-Eyed Monster* (a needle on a pillow)
> – *The Milky Way* (a row of milk bottles)
> – *For Men Only* (a pair of suspenders)

-For Women Only (a powder puff)
-Ruins in China (broken plates)
-Black Diamonds (coal)

"Well done!" I left at noon. The clubhouse sat on Little Lake. Pumpkin buoys. The dock onshore. Clockface gas pumps read zero.

* * *

Sundown I walked the downtown core. With Ivory I soaped curlicues on storefronts. I tossed rolls of toilet tissue into trees. I mashed apples into the street. With cookie cutters I punched faces in pumpkins, then slicked them with Vaseline, to prevent puckering.

A bum scrutinizing me. I stuffed straw up his sleeves and down his neck. I slipped a dollar in his pocket.

"Go get 'em, scarecrow."

* * *

"Our first trick-or-treater!" I said.
His name was Charlie. Charlie was Tom Mix:

holsters, chaps, Stetson. I patted his head. A shutterbug snapped us with infrared film. The flash was bluish. A bruise when I blinked.

"This is stupid," Charlie said.

"Spooky," I said.

The bakery dropped a gingerbread ghost in his pillowcase. The fabric store gave him candy corn wrapped in orange cloth. The confectioner was dressed as Jack the Sailor, the Crackerjack mascot. His staff wore silver foil doublets and elf slippers, *à la* Wrigley's Spearmint Spearmen.

The dentist handed Charlie a toothbrush.

"Stupid," Charlie said.

I conducted him into Creepy Clinic. Nurses from the local hospital were dressed as skeletons.

"This will ensure there are no glass shards or pins or other dangerous objects," I said, dumping goodies from Charlie's pillowcase onto a slab.

In ten minutes we had an X-ray. I handed it to Charlie.

"I don't want it," he said.

"Of course you do," I said. "Pretend it's a game. Hershey bars are ladders. Licorice are snakes."

THE BELL-RINGER

I came to in a field, head on the steering wheel. Fence rails on the hood.

"Shit." I fired up the engine, reversed over corn, headed east. Sky pinkening.

A sign whipped past: *PETERBOROUGH—11 MILES*.

* * *

A Gideon Bible and a Hollywood bed. The wallpaper yellow like the pits of my shirt.

I changed. Took supplies from my keister, arranged them in my gripsack—catalogues, order forms, trade cards. Each trade card featured a cut-out window in the shape of a blooming gladiolus. Behind each window was a colored wheel. Turn it and the glad turned red, then green, then yellow.

I sold glads in all shapes, sizes and shades. Sample bulbs came one per wax bag. Women preferred Lord Nelsons and George Washingtons. I packed some of each, plus Gorgeous Debs and Phantom Beauties. Old men went for those.

I stepped out. Down the hall every door was open. Drummers sitting in sample rooms, products piled on trunks. Stainless-steel potato peelers. Gold-plated pickle forks. Tiers of shoes, all rights, all size nines.

They nodded. I nodded back.

There was a ham-and-egger off the lobby. Steam from steam tables. I sat at the counter. A gripsack under every booth.

The fellow beside me opened his grip. Ten trays folded out, all of them empty.

"It's the ideal sample case," he said. "Comes in brown or black leather. You got your celluloid covers. You got your genuine aluminum trays, whatever size suits you. Guaranteed for twenty years."

In the barbershop I got a shave and a clip. Splashed smellgood on my suit.

Walked London Street. Dublin. Edinburgh.

A white clapboard hedged by lilacs. Some biddie answered the door.

"Would you be the green thumb of the house?" I said.

* * *

Hyacinths growing in boots, roses in tires.

"Hair," the man said. "And fingernails. God's own fertilizers."

"Ever try your locks on a Marshall gladioli?" I pulled out a catalogue. "All our flowers are prize-winners, our prices are very competitive—"

Needles in my neck. I weaved across the porch. Blacked out.

* * *

Came to on a gurney. A surgeon switched on a lightboard, tacked up an X-ray. Front view of my skull. It looked like half an apple. My nostrils were seeds.

A blotch on my brain.

"It's in a bad spot," he said. "The tumor. These blackouts will become more frequent."

I swung my legs off the gurney. "I've got places to be."

He pocketed my car keys. "I suggest you contact kin."

When he left I dressed. Stole down the stairwell. Silk roses in the gift shop. A marble Mary on the lawn. Sprinklers churred.

GRAB BAG

> *"Strangle Weed... is largely confined to the southern counties bordering on Lake Erie. During the last few years, however, it has been found growing and producing seed on farms near Peterborough..."*
> —The Weeds of Ontario, 1940

THE PITCHMAN

"Started with stems," the farmer said. "Millions of them. They spread out and wrapped around the clover. Then they sent out little yellow suckers. The suckers bored right into the clover."

I pitched hay from the crib, drayed it to the field. Spread it over the Strangle Weed. Clover dead beneath.

Barn to field, field to barn. All afternoon. When the hay was two feet high I waded through it, sloshing kerosene.

I struck a match. Fire sprouted.

"Six hours, six dollars," I said. "That was the deal."

The farmer flipped me a dollar. "Don't seem like you're in much of a position to dicker."

His son on the stoop. Hefting a Winchester sixteen-gauge.

Sun setting I tramped toward the town, blisters blossoming on my palms, shoulders, soles.

Spring wagons and trucks parked around the square. Farmers shooting the shit by the druggist's.

"Any of you looking for help?" I said.

"If you're working for free," one farmer said. Laughing.

I laughed. Then I slugged him. His nose folded over. His pals seized my arms. My jaw took a Coke bottle.

* * *

A nurse cracked the door. "There's a policeman who'd like to speak to you," she said.

Five-foot drop from clinic window to service alley. I ran through town. Sidewalk to ditch. Burs prickly as stitches. Milkweed swabs.

Train tracks crosscut the road. I followed them to a siding. Hid behind a pyramid of ties.

A train chugged in to water. When it chugged out I hopped a boxer.

"On the bum?" A man puffing a stogie. He pulled a bottle from his satchel, rolled it to me.

I struck a match.

DR. PEARSON'S GOLDEN MEDICAL DISCOVERY
Works through the stomach direct on the blood. Pimples, Boils, and other Skin Diseases are driven away.
DO NOT WAIT!
DELAY IS DANGEROUS!

I sniffed it.

"Hooch, kid," he said. "You won't feel no pain."

* * *

I picked weeds. Black Medick by a barn in Brantford. Beggar's Button between Strathroy and Stratford. Lindsay was flush with False Flax, Fleabane, Wild Vetch, Devil's Plague, Creeping

Charlie, Blue Bur, Wormwood, Wheat Thief, Graveyard Weed, Bastard-cress.

In Peterborough I bought bottles from a pharmacy, the one-drachm size. I took a room at the Y. I slit seed pods with my thumbnail.

* * *

"Sour risings?" I shouted. "Piles? Expectorations?"

A man with birdshit in his eyes.

"Fix cataracts lickety-split," I said, handing him a bottle. "Anti-scorbutic seeds."

King Devil seeds, actually. He paid fifty cents. Market Square. Farmers hawking veggies from buggies. I treated gout, dropsy, night sweats. Corn Cockle for corns. Orache for earaches.

"My head," a man said. "I black out."

I handed him Strangle Weed seed. "Boil it like tea and—"

He uncorked it, emptied it down his throat.

He gave me his wallet. His wedding ring. A hospital band. Then he wandered off. Head shaved. Barbicide sky.

THE CHUCK-SHOOTER

"Diamonds!" I said.

"Gypsum," he said. He worked for the government. He shone his flashlight and the walls twinkled. "Probably deposited by a subterranean stream. These walls show signs of water erosion."

We wormed along on our bellies. The tunnel sloped, then leveled out into a cave. We got up on all fours. He found arrowheads, a birch-bark bowl. Chill air seeping out from somewhere.

"Gold?" I said.

"Potassium nitrate," he said, spading the ground. "Used in fertilizers. Medicines. Saltpeter, for one. I'd like your permission to conduct a dig."

"Over my dead body!" I said.

* * *

"There's candles," I said. "A pot to pee in. Ring the cowbell if you think of something else."

The lady coughed and wrapped herself in blankets. The TB whipping her lungs.

"You'll be better in no time!" I said, inching out ass-first.

Up top it was dusk. Bats chipped the sky. I crossed the field to the cabin. Stacks of letters on the table. *URGENT,* they said. Or: *OPEN THIS ONE FIRST.*

I picked a purple envelope. "*Yes!*" the letter said. "*I want to be CLEANSED BY THE EARTH'S PURE AIR! I want to SLEEP ON A BED OF VITAMINS! I want to be CURED IN THE INDIAN MIRACLE CAVE!*"

All the hooey my ad said. I puffed into the envelope. A check wafted out.

* * *

His family drove up in the a.m. When I hollered the old guy clambered out of the cave.

"Your eyes?" a woman said.

"Never better!" he said, squinting at her. Squinting behind us. His face fell. "A bear!"

It was two cops. My pal from the government. He handed me a deed.

"This land doesn't even belong to you, does it?" he said.

* * *

I tramped around Smith township, up and down rural routes, till I seen it. Newspaper glued over the windows. I rapped the door and the door opened. There was two rooms. A smashed-up hope chest. Springs sticking like twisters from a bed.

"Home!" I said.

In the field I hunted caves. I found woodchuck holes, dozens of them. A woodchuck waddled out, twenty-pounder at sixty paces. I slingshot a stone. The woodchuck rolled to a den. I reached my arm down. I pulled hay out of the mouth. Soppy with blood. The more hay I pulled the further down the woodchuck rolled. Whimpering.

Next day I was in thistle, spines sticking my shins. I come on another woodchuck. He was flat on his back, huffing and puffing, nothing but fur and bones. I poured water on him. I stuck a bramble in his mouth. But his teeth were grown down past his chin. Too long to chew with.

I cracked his head on the side of the cabin. Stewed him up with dandelions.

* * *

"There's more where that come from," I said. I laid woodchucks face down on newspaper, slit them open, scraped off meat.

The butcher weighed it. "Ten cents," he said.

"That's farm-fresh!"

"Take it or leave it."

I took it. He ground the meat, mixed it with hamburger.

* * *

In his window the furrier had mannequins in mink jackets, squirrel capes, beaver wraps.

A lady made to go in.

"I got just the thing for you," I said. I slung a woodchuck hide around my neck and tucked the tail beneath the teeth. "It's a stole. A real furbelow."

The lady laughed, pushed past.

"A bathmat?" I said.

* * *

The woodchuck balanced on its back legs, forelegs wired together.

"We're talking big," I said. I shoved a cigar between his paws. "It holds your lighter, pipe, whatever."

The clerk led me down the aisle. He showed me ashtrays made of steel bowls glued to deer hoofs. Hat racks made of hoofs nailed to mounts. A moose-leg lamp base.

A row of squirrels, butane tanks up their butts, fuel lines inside, flints between their paws.

The clerk popped my cigar in his mouth, lit it off a squirrel.

I rode up the escalator to where they sold toys. "How's about this," I said, waving my woodchuck at a clerk. "Stick some candies down his throat, hang him from the ceiling, kids can bat him with a stick. What do you call those things?"

* * *

I hauled a woodchuck from the icebox. He was stuffed down a pair of stockings.

I flopped him on his stomach, slit down his back, slit around his tailbone and the claws. Skin peeled off his head like a sock. I yanked out his skull and spine. I sprinkled cornmeal on blood, to sop it up.

I mixed some cornmeal and water and ate dinner.

The body I made out of wood wool and glue. I slipped the hide over top. Starting at the tail I basted the back with fishing line. When I sewed the head his ears pricked up. I painted tar on his claws. I used iodine to redden his nose.

I carried him to the field, wedged his bottom in the mouth of a den. There was another woodchuck burrowing nearby. Two chomping thistles. One sniffing the air on a knoll.

I sprinkled arsenic on them. Arsenic's a preservative. I scythed the grass. I walked to the end of my drive.

VARMINT VILLAGE
50¢ ADULTS
10¢ FOR KIDS

* * *

I hitched a ride north.

"What're you hunting?" my ride said.

"A bear or a deer," I said. "Something big. For my attraction."

At Burleigh Falls I struck out into bush. Leaves turning. Birds kiting.

Something snapped. A flash of whitetail. I bird-dogged it. I trampled shoots, leapt logs. Branches jagged my face.

I spied hoof prints, droppings in the duff. I barreled down a hill and into a clearing. The prints ended. I sank calf-deep in bog. When I tried to get out I sank deeper. Knees, thighs, hips. Up to my armpits, grasping at moss. Screaming like a pie bird.

THE FIEND

I picked marijuana weed. I rolled it in corn husks. I squatted by the road, smoked a corn husk dube. Stashed a spare in my silverware case.

A car. I waved it down, whipped the door open. Old coot behind the wheel. "Where you headed?" I said.

"Peterborough."

I hopped in. "Got any grub?"

He shook his head, wrassled the gear stick. Liver spots on his hands.

"Yes sir, pretty soon I'm gonna be eating caviar," I said, knocking my case. "Once them city boys get a load of this baby I'll be set up good. Nobody's saw one of these before. Know what it is?"

The old coot shook his head.

"A home embalming kit," I said. "Say someone keels over, no doctor for miles. Or say you're in town and you don't wanna fork over an arm and a leg to some crepe-hanger. Know what I'm saying?"

His eyeballs bouncing: road, me, road, me.

I opened my case. Oak outside, red velvet in. I pointed to the skewers. "For when a stiff's skin sags," I said. "Then all you gotta do is bunch it together and pin it."

I touched behind his ear.

I pointed to a trochar. "For draining innards. Just poke it through the bellybutton. Makes a little fountain. Got that off a doctor. It's all rusted so he got himself a new one."

I pulled the scalpel out. The car swerved.

"Don't panic, Pops!" I said. "You ain't dead yet!"

I laughed, rubbed my belly. "And it ain't right yet. I've gotta get some rubber hosing, a bottle of formaldehyde. And face paint. I've gotta get some face paint. You know stiffs wear face paint? On their lips, cheeks, everywhere."

His face was white as whiskers.

"When you're dead your face gets all purple. So you got to make it pale, like yours. I was thinking lemon juice might do the trick. Save a few pennies."

I cracked my knuckles. "Thing is with these big-shot undertakers, they're just after money. They got this gizmo shoots wires into your jaw, to keep it shut. Why not sew the lips? Just baste 'em. Like turkeys.

"And they say, 'Oh, you gotta have spikes through your eyelids. You gotta have dry shampoo.' These guys ever hear of glue? Ever hear of egg yolks? I use 'em all the time, and my hair's all right. Eh?"

He nodded. I shut the case. Caught some Zs. Streetlamps woke me. Hunger pains. On the sidewalk a fellow roasting chestnuts in an oil drum.

Pops pulled over.

"Could you spot me two bits?" I said. "I'm good for it. Soon as I show them boys my kit I'll be flush—"

"Get out," he whispered. "Please."

I climbed out, belly cramped to hell, the smell of puffed wheat breezing down from the Quaker Oats plant. All down George St. folks was window-shopping. A string of sausages noosed in a butcher's. A stuffed grizzly in Lech's Furs.

I lit the other dube.

THE GLORY-ROADER

I stalked past Gloria's Dress Shop, Peterborough Jewelers, straight into Turnbull's Department Store. Directory numbered like a phrenological head. Cosmetics—organ of death.

Salesgirls flitting about. Fingernails scarlet. Eyelids violet. Lashes green.

I stopped one. "What's that on your mouth?"

"My lips?" she said. "That's Rachel Red Lip-Rouge by Blu-Bell. Were you looking for something for your girlfriend?"

"Do you know what's in that rouge?" I said. "Bugs. That rouge is made of carmine bugs which are from Mexico and which are dead. *Dead!*"

She backed away. "Security!"

"You got face cream on too?" I said. "Know what's in it? Whale seed! You think that's decent? You think that's Christian?"

A guard grabbed me. Chucked me out.

At Clark's Dry Goods I bought a tin of rat poison. I ducked back into Turnbull's. Past coffin-shaped counters. Lamps hunched like buzzards. I picked up a tester. Vanishing Cream. I shook a little poison in. Sliding down the counter I poisoned Skin Food and Skin Tonic, too.

"Stop!" The guard hollered from Hose.

I winged a jar at him. Hightailed it out the door. As I stepped off the curb a car slammed into me. For a second I heard nothing. Fluids trickling.

"Stand back!" Some guy knelt beside me. Black suit, straw hat fraying. Eyes glassy.

I tried to rise onto an elbow.

"I'll take care of this," he said. He pushed me down. Opened a silverware case. Pulled out a needle. He raised the thing up. Stabbed it through my stomach.

A lady shrieked. I crawled to the curb. Blood spurting from my navel, blood streaming out my nose. My spine shimmying. I lift my eyes heavenward. But the sky looked like an eye shadow sample. Black. Plum. Pink.

Derek McCormack's books include *Dark Rides, Wish Book,* and, most recently, *The Haunted Hillbilly.* He is the author of *Halloween Suite* and *Western Suit,* limited-edition chapbooks from pas de chance books. *Wild Mouse,* a carnival book he cowrote, was nominated for the Toronto Book Award. McCormack's journalism has appeared in such magazines and newspapers as *nest, Saturday Night,* and the *Globe & Mail.* His nonfiction has been nominated for a National Magazine Award in Canada. He lives in Toronto.

Printed in the USA
CPSIA information can be obtained
at www.ICGtesting.com
LVHW022041110824
787948LV00005B/573